BRIGHT SHARDS
— OF —
SOMEPLACE ELSE

FLANNERY
O'CONNOR
AWARD
FOR
SHORT
FICTION

Nancy Zafris,
Series Editor

BRIGHT SHARDS
— OF —
SOMEPLACE ELSE

STORIES BY MONICA MCFAWN

THE UNIVERSITY OF GEORGIA PRESS

ATHENS AND LONDON

© 2014 by the University of Georgia Press
Athens, Georgia 30602
www.ugapress.org
All rights reserved
Designed by Kaelin Chappell Broaddus
Set in 10/14.5 Kepler Std Regular
Manufactured by Sheridan Books, Inc.
The paper in this book meets the guidelines for
permanence and durability of the Committee on
Production Guidelines for Book Longevity of the
Council on Library Resources.

Printed in the United States of America
14 15 16 17 18 C 5 4 3 2 1

Library of Congress Cataloging-in-Publication Data
McFawn, Monica.
[Short stories. Selections]
Bright shards of someplace else : stories / by Monica McFawn.
pages cm. — (Flannery O'Connor award for short fiction)
ISBN-13: 978-0-8203-4687-8 (hardback : alk. paper)
ISBN-10: 0-8203-4687-X (hardback : alk. paper)
1. Short stories, American. I. Title.
PS3613.C4397B75 2014
813'.6—dc23
2013049714

British Library Cataloging-in-Publication Data available

CONTENTS

ACKNOWLEDGMENTS

Thank you to the journals that first published this work, occasionally in slightly different form: "Out of the Mouths of Babes," *Georgia Review*; "Dead Horse Productions," *Gargoyle*; "Elegantly, in the Least Number of Steps," *Confrontation*; "Improvisation," *Hotel Amerika*; "The Slide Turned on End," *Web Conjunctions*; "Ornament and Crime," *American Short Fiction*; "Line of Questioning," *Gettysburg Review*; "Snippet and the Rainbow Bridge," *Bellingham Review*; "The Chautauqua Sessions," *Missouri Review*; and "A Country Woman," *Passages North*. Thank you to all these journals and editors for their support. I also want to thank all the literary journals over the years that have declined my work with a complimentary note. These near misses were highly encouraging, and I appreciate the editors and readers who took the time to write to me.

I've also appreciated the good counsel and support of several people. I want to thank Anthony Doerr for his early insight and support of my short fiction and Christopher Stephens for his brilliance and antagonism—our aesthetic arguments have been a long-term fuel for my writing. I'm grateful to the Finnish Writing Group (Caitlin Horrocks, Beth Staples, Robby Taylor, Ben Drevlow, and Liz Weld) for their suggestions on several of these pieces. Both your comments and the fine examples of your own writing spurred me to make these stories better versions of themselves. I want to thank series editor Nancy Zafris for her insights, encouragement, and above-and-beyond advocacy for the work in this collection. I also appreciate the University of Georgia Press's care in creating a beautiful finished product.

I also want acknowledge those people and beings in my life who helped this book in a more indirect way. I'm indebted to my family for teaching me to see the value in whimsy and subversion. Thank you to all the horsewomen I've known who've shown me how to care passionately for something esoteric and impractical. And thank you to my two horses—Shamus Fancy and GG Eragon—who have taught me how to trust myself in the act of trusting them. And thanks to Bob Marsh, for showing me, through his stellar example, how to live as an artist.

BRIGHT SHARDS
— OF —
SOMEPLACE ELSE

OUT OF THE MOUTHS OF BABES

He was nine years old. He had eczema. He scored very high on all tests that measured verbal ability. Some teachers mistook his brilliance for a smart mouth. Flossing was a point of contention, sometimes. He had a special diet—be sure to follow the special diet. He was different. A different child.

Grace had learned all this about the boy, Andy, in the first few moments of setting foot inside the Henderson household. Much could be made of the order in which the mother listed the boy's traits. He was a young rash, an articulate and bratty rash, a high-maintenance and oh-so-special rash. Grace nodded as if everything the mother was saying was perfectly logical and expected. The boy sat across from her, playing a hand-held video game and sucking from a silver juice bladder. He pulled the straw from the juice and used it to scratch his head, then put it back.

"What was that again?"

"I said, keep him off the phone. He doesn't need to be on the phone today."

The mother gathered up her bags, turned to her son, and smiled. Grace would see a usual range of looks from parents during this moment: the clingy ones would blink all misty-eyed; the ragged ones would flash a guilty smile, ashamed at their own relief; the boastful parents would give a kind of wink, imagining all the ways the nanny would soon be dazzled. But when this mother met her boy's eyes, she visibly shrank in her suit as if caught in a compromising moment. The boy looked up from his game and gave his mother a tight smile—the thin courtesy a person gives a beggar who is thanking him too profusely.

The silver car backed out of the driveway, the late-afternoon light flashing off its hood. The boy shielded the game screen with his hand and kept on playing. Grace watched him for a moment. He was sandy haired, with a high rosiness on his cheeks that looked like misapplied blush. His irises, under a frill of tufted lashes, were dappled gray-green like Spanish moss shot through with sun. She considered greeting him, or hunkering down next to him and asking about his game, but thought better of it. She hated the awkward joviality that always marked the first one-on-one discussion with a child, so lately she had skipped it altogether. She had all evening with the boy—the mother would be out late on a catering job—so there was no need to hurry things along.

She began her tour. The mother had shown her around the house —here's the pantry, here's the laundry, be careful about this lock, it needs a hard turn, hold down the handle for a second or two to flush—but she always made her own circuit when the parents left. She enjoyed seeing how people arranged their things, found a comfort in the contents of other people's medicine cabinets—those little curios of weakness and disease; she liked noticing the things that had been done for her first-day benefit (toys stuffed under the bed, fanned magazines on the coffee table, fresh soap in the dish) and the things that had gone undone (the rusty sink drains, dirty panties at the top of the laundry pile). She popped her head in the master bath, ran her hands over the couple's bed, then stepped into the boy's room and looked around. The twin bed was neatly made, and books rather than toys filled the shelves. The only concession to whimsy was a stylized bear painted on the wall, its paw in an abstract-expressionist honey pot composed with loose strokes.

The boy was an only child, it appeared. The third bedroom was used as a study, full of dark shelves and dressers. She particularly liked going through drawers. Funny that it was a pleasure, she thought, as she pulled the small brass knocker on the first set of drawers. As a child she had found troubling things: a note from her father to a mistress ("I want to dwell in the minute I first see you"), a bizarre letter that her mother had been long drafting to her own father, the handwriting and mood changing over the course of six pages. When she held these unhappy documents in her hands, the aired secrets seemed to make the silent room buzz. Mostly, though, she found nothing of interest, either in her childhood home or the homes of strangers. The act of opening drawers soothed her in ways she couldn't place. She wasn't looking for scandal or valuables; she just liked looking.

The first drawer was filled with pens and office supplies, the second with tax documents and receipts, the third with framed photographs that had made their way out of rotation. One was of the boy, perhaps three years old, pulling a toy wooden boat through a greasy puddle. He regarded the camera with an aggressive look of inquiry, like a professor about to put a difficult question to an unprepared class. With his free hand he pointed to an appliquéd patchwork turtle on the front of his sweatshirt, as if it were a visual for the coming lecture. She was about to reach for another frame when she heard a man's voice from downstairs. Startled, she shoved the picture back in the drawer and stood up. Was it a delivery man? Had the boy let him in?

As she walked down the stairs, she began to make out what was being said. "Mmmm . . . I see. But what if we have wood termites? You'd just leave and treat them on a second visit?" When she entered the living room, she was surprised to see only the boy: he was on the phone and the voice was coming from him. His back was turned to her and she stopped to listen. "That doesn't work. What if they multiply in between the two visits? Then you'll get more money than if you treated for them the first time through."

The boy, when she listened more closely, didn't sound like a man, exactly. His words began with an eager high chirp and a fuzzy pronunciation, like those of most children, but the ends of his phrases were crisp, even brittle. Within a single sentence he ran through the vocal life cycle, sounding like both a babbling toddler and an old man with the bass thinned out from his tone. The person on the other end of the line would have a hard time suspecting his age, not in the least because of his apparent penchant for hard bargaining. "No, I need all the vermin taken care of in one go. I have in my hand a coupon from your competitor—Riddit—and it says here that they'll . . ." The boy was getting more and more excited. She could see him bounce on the couch as he read out the coupon in a ringing, triumphant voice. "Okay, then. I look forward to getting the manager's call." He hung up the phone and caught sight of her.

"Have a vermin problem?" she asked, seating herself in the loveseat across from him. He looked like any other kid in the face, obstinacy mixed up with vulnerability.

"I don't know if we do. But I want to find the best deal just in case. I like to practice."

"Practice what?"

"Negotiating." He pronounced each syllable of the large word and smiled at the sound of it.

"Did your mother ask you to find a deal on an exterminator?"

"No. But that doesn't matter. It doesn't matter if I talk to salespeople; they're paid to talk." The mention of his mother seemed to put them on bad footing. Grace leaned back in the loveseat and sighed. An easily affronted child—the smarter ones always were. She decided she wouldn't say a thing more. Let him wonder if she was going to tattle on him to his mom. She was thirsty, anyhow. She pulled herself up and wandered into the dining room, soon finding herself in front of a large, gleaming liquor cabinet under a sideboard. There were all kinds of fancy snifters, highball glasses, cut crystal servers and decanters, but she made up her drink—vodka on the rocks—in an orange Tupperware cup. She had lately taken to having her first earlier and earlier, since otherwise she'd spend too much of the evening planning and wondering about the best time to make it. To have the drink in her hand, she thought, was to banish it from her mind. She took a long draw and refilled the cup—to save a return trip—and went back in to check on the boy.

He stared at the phone and she stared at him.

"The manager," the boy finally said. "He was supposed to call right back."

Andy was wearing a shirt with a clutch of tiger cubs screen-printed on the front, and he kept pulling it down as if it were riding up. His mouth was smeared red from a rash or the juice, and his bangs covered one eye. They both looked at the phone for a few moments before Grace spoke up.

"You know, if you want to negotiate on the phone, I've got something better for you than an exterminator."

"What? Are you going to trick me into calling my mom or some special kids' therapy hotline?"

Grace chuckled. She liked how he already knew the games a grownup might play. "No, no. I don't see anything wrong with you talking on the phone. I was impressed with what I overheard. How would you like to make an even tougher call?"

The boy nodded, wide-eyed, as if shocked at being indulged.

"Just give me one second. Let me give you the information you need."

Grace walked to the foyer and dug her cellphone bill out of her purse. With all that was going on, she hadn't had a chance to get those overage charges removed. She hated making such calls and always fell for the representative's tricks and runarounds, buying new products and features and even thanking those perky voices, when she hung up, for screwing her over. Let the boy wander into that maze of automated voices, menu options, on-hold music. He could defend her money from the call-center monster; it would be like one of his little video games. If nothing else, the call would keep him busy for at least an hour or so, leaving her free to call Greg and see what new dirt he'd dug up on Susan.

The foyer adjoined the dining room, so she swung off, refreshed her drink, and reentered the living room from the other side.

"Alright, Andy. Here's my bill. Here's my customer code. The last four digits of my social security number are 7419." She sat down on the couch by him and laid out the documents as if they were a board game. "They're going to ask you for all that. Then they'll ask you how they can help. Here's where you need to be sharp. You're going to ask them to take these charges off." She pointed to a line of numbers. The boy was transfixed and seemed to be holding his breath. He stared at the bill the way most boys his age would stare at pile of Legos, perhaps imagining all the configurations the call might take. Grace noticed his ears were bent down at the tips, as though he had not yet unfolded from the womb. There was no way he would get past the main menu, she thought.

Harmless fun. Still, she explained why the charges weren't fair, and for good measure let him in on some further injustices in her own grownup world. "I have to call a lot of lawyers. They charge me just for talking to them on the phone, and then the phone company charges me, too! Can you believe it?" She laughed.

"Are you in legal trouble?" The boy looked at her. His face was bland and rosy like any little kid's, but his eyes actually reminded her of her lawyer, J. T. Hillman, Esq.—the same sharp look, the pinprick of a pupil that would pop any of your bullshit before it even formed in your head. She'd have to be straight with the boy.

"We'll get to that. Are you ready to call now, or do you need some review time?"

In answer, he dialed. For a while they were both silent. She could hear the hold music muffled by the child's ear. He let out a deep breath and squeezed his eyes shut, but then his face softened and took on a meditative look. He pressed a few buttons with great precision and a bit of flourish, like a pianist. Grace watched him and sipped her drink.

This wasn't nice, what she was doing. He would get frustrated. He might tell his mother. No, he wouldn't do that; she had enough leverage with the exterminator call. They had achieved that equilibrium where she had something on him and he something on her.

"I have a problem with some charges on my bill," he began. His voice rang out with a compelling combo of childish eagerness and unmistakably adult impatience. Grace tensed up. Suddenly, she didn't want to be there to witness the eroding of his innocent confidence. She stood up, wandered into the dining room, and checked her voice-mail. Greg had left a message. After he got through baby-talking to her, she heard what he had found out about her sister:

"Baby, I dug through everything. She is as clean as a whistle. A plowed snowdrift—nothing like her sis. Anyway, I stayed up all night and finally found, in the expunged crime record of Henry County, a charge for misdemeanor embezzling. She stole from Girl Scouts. Does that ring a bell?"

Grace shut the phone and topped off her drink. So that's all he found. Her sister Susan, four years her junior, was suing her for about ten grand, money that their mother had *not* left to Susan, who contended that their mother had not been lucid when she drew up the version of the will that favored Grace, and that Grace had manipulated their mother into excising Susan from the will. This was all true; Grace had done just that. Her mother had thought, in her addled state, that the newly drawn-up will was a petition for freeing the whales from Sea World.

But Grace and Susan had been feuding so long that everything could be framed as a justifiable retaliation. Their bad blood predated everything. Susan stole her boyfriends, turned relatives against her, tried to get her involuntarily committed. Grace had come back with restraining orders, countersuits, and most recently had hired a private investigator to find dirt. She was disappointed with Greg's find.

He was no better an investigator than he was a lover, apparently. Still, the private Catholic girls' school Susan worked at might be troubled by the Girl Scout thing. She stirred her drink and began rehearsing, under her breath, what she might say on Susan's voicemail. "St. Victoria's might be interested to learn that their 2000 Administrator of the Year awardee hasn't always been so upstanding . . ." Ugh. Thin gruel. It would take more than that to rattle Sue.

The boy was—remarkably—still on the phone when Grace returned. He was scribbling on her bill and his expression was that of Renaissance cherub. He beamed and chuckled into the receiver. She could hear a woman's warm voice trilling a laugh. "I'm so glad we had this talk," the boy said, convincingly earnest, chewing on the pen cap. His lacy eyelashes quivered, and he rubbed the underside of his nose with his index finger, playing his nostrils like a fiddle. "Bye now." He set the phone on its charger so softly it didn't make a click, then pulled up his empty juice box and did a staccato slurp on the straw.

"Well? How'd it go?"

"I got the charges off the bill. And I redid your contract so you now have unlimited minutes and it'll cost less than what you were already paying."

"Really?" Grace figured the boy was lying or simply confused. No way could the boy have done what he'd said.

"Really. And it wasn't even hard. It was boring. Kid stuff." He sneezed into his sleeve. "The representative started talking to me about her life and her kids and junk. Her name's Tracy and she said my call made her day." He squeezed the juice bladder in his fist. "You can call the automated system and check if you don't believe me. It's okay if you don't believe me. Most people don't. I won't be mad."

Grace studied the boy. She wanted him to see that she wasn't just another skeptical, unimaginative adult. She was different.

She *felt* different, alright. Her cup seemed to have lightened to the point that it was floating off her hand, pulling her arm up with it. Why did she suddenly care what the kid thought?

"I believe you," she began, lurching toward the phone with her cup held above both of them. "But I'm going to check anyhow." She pressed redial and hit the menu buttons while the boy watched like a master observing a fumbling apprentice; he whispered "just hit zero" when she accidentally got to the wrong part of the menu and had to start over to get to her billing statement. A sensual and robotic voice reported in perfect deadpan that the boy had done it. Zero on her balance and forty dollars per month.

"Wow, kid . . . color me impressed." She was now sitting next to him on the couch, the phone between them on the cushion. He had grabbed his video game again and his thumbs twitched on the buttons with what seemed to her a virtuosity. She had been really dreading making that call, and now it was all taken care of, just like that. This small relief was like a shot of clean oxygen in a deep cave. "Andy," she began. "Would you like to make another call?"

"Only if it's tougher."

"It's tougher. I owe some money. A few thousand, in fact. I need you to see if you can get the interest charges off the debt."

"Who do you owe?"

"I owe some money to Firekeeper's Casino. I have a credit card with them. I lost some money playing slots. I think there was something wrong with the machines that day, or something. Usually I can just watch the lights and the fruit and get a payout pretty regularly. I have a system. This one night the same two bananas and a cherry kept coming up. Maybe you could say there was a glitch."

She was lying about the banana and cherry thing, but not about her system. Typically she did get a payout, although she had to admit that her system usually involved simply getting blitzed and pulling from a five-gallon bucket full of tokens at her feet. The servers and staff would all whistle when she came in with the bucket, and the other gamblers—those who were tourists and not locals, so to speak—might turn and look at her like she was something more real, in that context, than they were. The rest of the herd didn't look up.

To her credit, the bucket was never actually full. She filled the bottom with several hotel-bar-sized bottles of wine and liquor, covered them with a tin pie plate, then topped it off with tokens. She wasn't about to blow her money on the house's pricey drinks, so all night she would feed the slots and surreptitiously fill up her red plastic cup. She'd watch the fruit and the lights and get to feeling that she was decoding a language every time she pulled the handle. When the payout came, it was like she'd been speaking pidgin to an uncomprehending foreigner and had suddenly achieved fluency. The dings and bells told her she had made herself understood.

"I don't think that would work," the boy said. "And why were you gambling so much? The odds of those machines are, like, really bad."

Grace had to expect some judgment, she figured. She had lost thousands over the years. She had little left for legal fees and nothing left of her mother's inheritance. She wasn't above prostrating herself in front of the boy, if that's what it took to get the job done.

"What can I say? I'm stupid. I mean, you get a payout so you keep playing. Sometimes I don't know when to fold 'em, as they say. But there are people a lot worse off than I am."

"Just because people are worse off doesn't mean you aren't bad." He seemed to consider his own words. "I guess I should say 'no offense.' So, no offense."

"None taken. Hey, we all make mistakes. I'm sure you get in fights with your little friends or steal their crayons sometimes." She sucked down the last of her drink, then picked the now-tiny ice cubes from her cup and pressed them into the dirt of a potted plant on the side table.

"I don't get in fights with friends because there are none to fight. And I don't use crayons. Colored pencils give a lot better control."

Should she latch onto the friend comment and try to find some deeper emotional ground with the boy? Or was it best to just roll on past? The house and the mother told the story: this unusual, cloistered boy no doubt lived a solitary life, too precocious for his peers and too young for any adults to take seriously. She could tell him that she, too, considered herself an outsider, with few allies in the world and even fewer friends. But why draw attention to that? Better to just give him the phone. The call would offer him an escape from his circumscribed life as a boy-genius; that was better than the two of them moaning about loneliness. She ruffled his hair with awkward affection; her hands, wet with ice, got nicely dry in his blond mop.

"I hear you. I'm a colored pencil girl, all the way. Try drawing an eyeball with a crayon! Ready?"

The boy nodded, and again she laid out the relevant information. Grace jumped up from the couch as he began dialing. She paced around the first floor, hearing snippets of his progress ("Can I speak to a manager?") and debating about whether she needed another drink. She popped the cork from a small bottle of port and escaped her indecision. She returned to the boy and sat across from him; he was in the midst of a monologue:

"You could get into my notes page and erase the earlier records on my account so no one would know what you did. You could also do the opposite and rack up my bill. I think your job would be fun, Jim, for these reasons." The boy's voice, this time, sounded higher and oddly husky, like female smoker trying to baby talk. He spoke quickly and laughed a bit, a charmingly nervous sound that threaded through his words and made everything he said a sweet half-joke. "Oh, so it's not fun . . . just in a call center. I guess if I were you I'd want to do something crazy now and again. But I'm already a bad gambler. So I shouldn't propose stuff like that." He paused and pulled the phone away from his ear and held it out at arm's length. This struck Grace as a showboating gesture, as if he were a cyclist weaving through traffic no-handed. The voice on the phone—Jim—let loose a stream of corporate gibberish into open air, but the boy didn't appear to be listening. He pulled the straw from his juice and gnawed on it. In a slow, smooth motion, he wound the phone back to his ear and said a few garbled and urgent words into the mouthpiece.

Another long pause, and then "No, of course not . . . no more than five or six times, tops . . . As a matter of fact, yes . . . She plays volleyball? The sport of princesses!"

The thread was lost on Grace, but she felt hypnotized by the boy's tone, the widening of his eyes, the small, polished giggles, the cajoling followed by a sudden cold word, which crackled like ice dropped in a hot toddy. Andy was talking on the phone, but she felt his disjointed comments were making an appeal to her personally. For what, she couldn't say, but she was starting to feel different—yes, her head was swimming, but that wasn't different, not really—she felt, watching him, that he was, with his little-boy claw hands, ripping a hole in a heavy scrim that long lay between her and the rest of the world. She was, she felt, surfacing. But she was also getting the bends.

The boy sat Indian-style on the couch cushions, his fluffed-up hair forming a perfect looping curl, like a bent horn, right on the top of his head. In another place and time a boy like him would be trussed up in velvets and dripping gold tassels and paraded through the town on a platform carried high by elders, and as he passed her on the street she would hope simply to catch his eye, or—better yet—to hear him speak. Or maybe she would trek to him, as he sat in the center of a donut of fog high on a precipice. Tell me, oh wise one . . .

She laughed to herself; he was just a kid, whatever that meant. He laid down the phone and said, simply, "Done."

"You did it."

"Yup. Easy-peasy. It's all about what you do and don't say, and I know when to shut up and when to speak. It's like a game."

"You're amazing. Just, wow." The boy had lifted another burden off her as if unhooking a balloon from its bunch to sail away. A giddiness rose up in her, and she looked around for something to distract her from a manic laugh. On the side table, she spotted the mother's list. *Eczema cream twice nightly. No liquids after nine. Make sure he uses floss and gets the uppers* and *the lowers . . .*

Grace stood up and floated into the bathroom. The cream bore a piece of masking tape marked "Andy." The tube was solid in her hand, fraught; it was one of the boy's things. She returned and presented it to him on her outstretched palms.

"You've got to apply this," she said, and he plucked it from her and squeezed a pearl into his hand. He anointed his inner elbow with what she now recognized as characteristic grace, and she knew the night was back onto appropriate footing: the responsible au pair and the obedient child.

"Is that all you have?" Andy said.

"You have to floss at some point, too."

"I mean, all the calls you have?"

Of course she had more calls! A problem for every call and a call for every problem—she could think of another one right now. But it wasn't the kind of call he could make.

"It's not the kind of call you could make."

"Why not? Does it have to do with your legal stuff?"

"Sort of. And other, personal stuff. It wouldn't be strictly a company call."

"I can make all kinds of calls."

"Well, I'd have to give you more background and you'd really have to listen."

"Okay."

She could not really let him make this call, but she saw no harm in laying out, as a form of bedtime story, just what kind of shit she was in. In that spirit she went to the kitchen, where she made up a cup of warm milk and honey for the boy and a milky drink for herself—one of those creamy liqueurs that were normally served hot and topped with whipped cream and sprinkles, though she now just zapped it for thirty seconds in the microwave. She brought the drinks into the living room and turned off all the lights but the one next to them. Then, she began.

She started out telling her story in clear, picture-book sentences, the kind that are one to a page. "There were once two sisters," she said, and in her mind's eye she saw the idyllic accompanying picture—a washed-out pastel of two sisters swinging on a tire swing over a blue-ribbon stream. "They were the best of friends," she continued, conjuring another picture—this time of the two of them laughing and giggling as they hid under the clothing racks while their mother yelled in a panic over their heads. Those storybook illustrators weren't good at panic, though. Maybe the girls could be pushing one of those big circle things, like kids from a bygone era. Maybe the story worked better in a different time period.

"Is this a real story?"

"Of course."

"Then why are you telling it like that? Those circle things are called trundle hoops, anyway."

She was on the wrong track here, somehow. The call wasn't about her history with her sister; he didn't need to hear about all that. It was about Greg. Nearly every romantic relationship she'd had in the last five years had come from the situation with her sister. She'd dated lawyers, of course, but also mediators (when they tried that), court staff, even former employees of her sister. Now she was seeing Greg, the private investigator. When she first met him he was attractive because he seemed to have the power to get her free. He was that rope cast down to her in the pit. But soon enough he, like the rest of them, became just another part of the problem, just another part of what she simply referred to in her mind as "Susan." The word no longer conjured up a person, but a constellation of bills to pay, appointments to make, paperwork to fill out, and moves demanding response. *Susan* was a word for the wild rudder of her life that she had to counteract daily at the helm. Greg was now part of Susan.

She began telling the boy all this, sketching out the feud and the lawsuit and Greg's poor performance as an investigator and how she had gotten involved with him for the "wrong reasons," and that now she wanted to fire him and dump him in the same brisk call. This would be tough, she explained, because fired employees and dumped boyfriends often wanted explanations. She didn't like explaining herself but always felt herself doing it, ad nauseam. Plus, Greg had a funny way of moving his upper lip that reminded her of the lower fringe of a jellyfish, undulating and curling in. He changed the way he walked based on who was watching. When he spoke he sounded intelligent but had a bovine look in his eye that made her doubt the existence of his soul. She wished there were a special kind of radio that would tune in to other people's thoughts, even for just a minute. She'd pay a mint for that. When she was a kid sometimes she thought she could hear Susan's thoughts when the two of them were falling asleep in their bunk beds. The moment was like a crossed-wire connection, and Susan's thoughts were always about the social situation between the fish in their fish tank.

Grace ranged wildly in her talk to the boy. She felt, sometimes, that he was the perfect confidant—mature enough to understand, young enough not to have his insight clogged up with learned falsehoods. At those moments she talked to him like a man. Other times he seemed more like a dog or cat, some questionably sentient being to whom she could spew her thoughts without concern about judgment or even comprehension. She spoke in that vaguely doubting way pet owners confided in their pets, then stopped to giggle at how silly she sounded. Or she sometimes spoke to him like an object, a key stuck in a lock, and in these cases she mumbled to herself about him while looking at him: *Stop it. Stop. He's just a little boy, you shouldn't be talking to him this way.*

She slumped on the couch. It was dark outside and she stared at the orange bottom of her cup, which caught the lamplight and reflected a small sun on her hand. The cup probably wasn't even microwave safe.

"Okay, is that all? Can I call now?"

"You can't. Don't you see? The guy's my employee and boyfriend. It's a call I have to make."

"Why? I could say I'm your new boyfriend. Or new investigator. Or best friend. Or representative. I've been my own father on the phone before and called about the treatment of myself at school. I've said stuff like 'He's a good kid, just weird,' because I know that's how it's said. I can do anything. Plus you don't even like the guy. So it doesn't matter."

Something needed correcting in the boy's logic, she knew, but she didn't feel moved to do it. She looked out the large picture window behind him. The driveway was lit up by small recessed lights pressed into the shorn lawn. It was raining, and the drive looked, through the distortion, like a bridge twisting in the wind. She remembered seeing an old black-and-white clip of a concrete bridge snapping like a jump rope before throwing off its burden of cars and souls. Something about the image made her take heart: that a solid bridge could get so loopy had good implications, she thought, and the silent, forgotten deaths made her feel she'd dodged a nasty bullet just by being born in a later age. The wind made the rain sluice down the window at all angles. The thin, wet trails all seemed to converge behind the boy's head, making him seem the center of a web—or an incredible deal that all arrows were pointing toward, a pattern of emphasis familiar to her from the neon signage that so often lit up her repetitive nights.

"You're right. Go for it. I'll pay him for his work, but I want out. Get me out."

The boy cracked his knuckles like an old pool shark and made the call. Grace could hear Greg announce his company name in a harangued voice, as if he had been fielding nonstop calls, though Grace knew that was a put-on. She fell back against the couch cushions, kicked her shoes off, and lay down. The throw pillows smelled like potpourri—lilac and geranium, a steamy whiff of green.

The smell transported her to the dank crawl space in her mind where all her out-of-rotation bitter memories were stored. (The more contemporary ones were on display right behind her eyes.) There, her eyes fell on a bouquet of nettles, dandelions, milkweed, and some spiky yellow flower that grew by the drainage ditches hemming her childhood lawn. She had built the bouquet for her Girl Scout pastime badge, and the flowers she had chosen were supposed to be both aesthetically pleasing and calling to mind the arrangement of character traits a young scout should exemplify. The other girls had chosen daisies for sweetness, roses for fidelity, petunias for perseverance, and the dull like. Grace's bouquet, she explained, expressed the critical qualities of defensiveness, invasiveness, passivity, and squalor.

The bouquet did not go over well. The troop leader pulled her aside and accused her of undermining the spirit, if not the letter, of Girl Scout Law. The other girls' blank sincerity was thrown up in her face as if she alone had flung open the door to all the forces of ambiguity that would soon enough sully their innocence for good.

When Grace had told Susan about this—at dinner, when their mother and father were arguing and deaf to their talk—little Susan had said a shocking and perfect thing: "She's a cuntbug." Cuntbug. The word had moved Grace profoundly. "Cunt" was a word they shouldn't have heard—lewdly adult. But "bug" commandeered the expression into a realm of childhood whimsy, a place that was far more ecstatically dark than anything a grownup could dream up. She loved her evil little sister then.

One of Grace's arms draped over the couch and grabbed the empty air, searching for her drink or perhaps simply arranging weeds in her dream at the edge of the carpet. She moaned and shifted, then sat bolt upright and cried out, in a voice rent by epiphany: "She embezzled from *Girl Scouts!*"

The boy put his nibbled straw to his lips in a shushing motion and then said into the phone, "She's shouting because of how lame that discovery is. It's second-class work."

But her mind was on fire. Susan had stolen from Girl Scouts. Was this not an act of love? Grace's heart was pounding through her body. She leaped up with her orange cup and went to the liquor cabinet for another drink, slopping gin all over the sideboard. She took a clarifying chug. This discovery felt like a communiqué. It sounded absurd, but Grace couldn't help but thinking that Susan had somehow arranged to have her find out about the embezzlement. This was, she felt, an olive branch, presented in the only way possible. Susan could not call her outright, what with all the restraining orders and pending court dates. The only way she could reach out to Grace would be to plant a clue—a loving clue, tied to a memory when they were aligned against something together—somewhere out in the mess for Grace to find.

When she returned to the living room and saw the boy hang up the phone, she already knew that Greg was out of the picture. She felt it in her bones—or, rather, she felt the lead shot of worry in her bones discharge, leaving her as light as a child's balsa plane.

"Greg's gone. I made sure. He wanted me to tell you that you're being shortsighted. I said, sure thing, private eye. He didn't get it. So dumb."

"I've got another—"

"Nah. I think I'm done." He squirmed into the corner of the couch.

"Wait. Just wait." The boy hadn't eaten—the normal dinner hour had long passed. She stepped toward the kitchen as if following a strange choreography—one foot shooting out in a wide side-step, the other in a heel-scraping jazzy thrust. It was the dance of staying upright. When she got to the refrigerator she opened it, clung to the handle, and spied the boy's sober dinner—a gluten-free enchilada and greens—among the fresh veggies, soda water, and cheese wheels. She could not serve such a thing to him. It would be dispiriting.

She thought of a gambler she once saw at the slots, a fat nobody slug who, by dint of his hot streak, became a kind of temporary god. Friends and hangers-on brought him meatloaf in Styrofoam, drinks, crab cakes, pudding . . . it went on and on into the night. If he moved, it was understood, the streak would end. It was also understood that these offerings of cake and meat were really being laid at the feet of Lady Luck, who was at that moment making herself manifest in that bloated husk.

She found a piece of old cherry cheesecake in tinfoil and a can of whipped cream tucked behind a stand of low-fat salad dressings. She snapped off several single-serve Jell-Os from a pack. High in a cabinet, she found a bag of chocolate baking chips. Under the stove, she found a deep roasting pan. She filled it with her finds and topped it off with a few travel bags of potato chips and some Lifesavers she dug out from her purse. She laid the feast at his feet. "Eat," she murmured. "Then we'll talk."

He pulled up the bag of chocolate chips by the corner and studied it. "This isn't my normal dinner," he said, "but that's okay."

She had figured the boy's powers of disentanglement came from an ascetic temperament, a personality naturally averse to the complications that came from any great pleasure, be it food or (one day) gambling or sex or whatever. But he had no trouble digging in. He ripped open the Jell-O pods, topping them with whipped cream. He unwrapped the Lifesavers and placed a chocolate chip in each opening and dunked the potato chips in the cheesecake as if it were a dip. He was both avid and precise, enjoying the treats fully but with an admirable sense of proportion. He didn't shake out the chocolate chip bag when he was finished to conjure a final morsel, but neither did he leave anything behind. (She checked.) God, he was so wise. She watched him from the couch, squirted whipped cream in her mouth, and swallowed it down with a hard sound, like a frightened character in a cartoon. Then she outlined the final call.

The boy listened gravely to her instructions, a golden shred of Jell-O trembling on his lips. He nodded and looked at her in quiet assessment, the way someone will check a dish he is scouring to see if it has come clean or needs another dunk. As the phone rang at the other end of the line, Grace reached out a limp hand in muted protest. She half-wanted him to hang up. But the boy was smiling. She heard Susan's voice, so much like her own, answer with a loud, startled hello, as if she were drunk. No surprise there. Once Grace dated a contractor who built kitchen cabinets for Susan and got to hear all about Susan's habit of changing the plan based on what was in her cup. "She wanted pine when she was drinking a pale ale, walnut when she was having a Guinness, and stainless steel when she was drinking vodka..."

The boy began speaking. "I'm calling on Grace's behalf."

And then he tangled with her. Boy, did he. Grace sat on the edge of the couch, knocking back her drink—a fresh one had appeared of its own volition, sensing that things were getting festive. First he soothed her with a string of careful little platitudes, words as smooth as bath beads: "there's no pressure," "you're entitled to your feelings," "darkest before dawn," "easy now." Then, while playing with the webbing between his toes, he rolled out an aggressive opening gambit, a double-jeopardy thingamajig—or was that a catch-22?

"If two people have restraining orders against each other," he lectured into the mouthpiece, "then they can meet without a problem, since they will both be violating the restraining order to the same degree. So to report the violation, in that situation, would be to report yourself." Grace couldn't get within fifty feet of Susan and Susan couldn't get within fifty feet of her, but if they both approached each other, say, in a public place, like at a certain fountain Grace knew with a cherub pissing recycled slurry in perpetuity, then they were safe. Come to think of it, the boy reminded her of that cherub, minus the profane spout; as he talked his eyes were uplifted in blissed-out relief, as if he were letting out a stream of something too long bottled up.

Andy was making short work of Susan. She could see it in the way he grinned and showed his squat baby teeth, like old gravestones sunk in soil. She could see it in the way he gleefully kicked the couch cushions—a boy revving up a playground swing. He was a prodigy... that he was. Grace had given him her worst to deal with, and he waved his hands over it and there it went. A popped bubble. A steamed-out stain.

The couch beneath her chin was chocolate-smeared, and a Lifesaver was stuck to the pillow. Lots of cleaning up to do before the mama bear comes home, she thought, and lay down, nestling her drink into the deep-pile, sea-foam carpet. She snapped one eye open to keep it on the boy. An alien sound issued from the phone—her sister's laugh. When had she last heard it? They had been passing each other in the courthouse, and Grace had tripped in her heels as she was turning to give Susan a cold look of reptilian indifference, a look ruined when she went down on one knee while J. T. Hillman, Esq., flapped his hands over her like a bird startled off his perch. Susan had laughed then—a sound that bounced off the marble steps and high ceiling, that pinged around in Grace's head exclusively and often. The old laugh and the new played off each other like fancy music with diverging motifs, the sort of music a pair of neighbor sisters, goody-goody brats, used to practice in their backyard on their piccolo and flute while she and Susan tried to hit their instruments with rotten apples from above.

By noon tomorrow the two of them would stand before the gushing cherub. Grace would throw in a penny or two while she waited. Love and embezzlement. Amen and goodnight.

The boy was off the phone now and leaning over her. "Thank you, thank you, thank you," she chanted, lifting her arms as if to pull him in for a pat on the head or a kiss. He was smiling at her but out of reach. His cheeks were flushed and his whole head, even the downy hair, had a heavy-bright look, like hand-colored black-and-white film. A candy knocked around in his mouth.

Her days of nannying had given her a taste for the vividness of children, the potency of those little dominoes ready to tip in a snaking line of lifelong complication. But the boy ran it in reverse, as if he had been born foreseeing all the complications and all the ways out. Above her head he made a wide arc with his arms and brought his fingers slowly together, meeting between her eyes at the exact midpoint. "You and Susan will meet like so. Approach at the same pace."

"Wow. Thank you . . . can't believe it . . . that's something else . . ."

Her words faded and she shut her eyes. She was spent. A wrapper crinkled and she smelled fruity, humid breath. The boy pressed two Lifesavers on her closed lids. The couch lurched like an old boat being kicked away from the shore.

He spoke with an easy gallows chatter, a clean, perky voice on the dark stream: "My father is a systems analyst, and my mother caters parties. I've solved their problems, made all the calls. Even called my mom for my dad and my dad for my mom and patched things up. It was cake. I think I am their last problem, the one they traded for all the others. I've sat at the phone for their benefit and talked to myself, explaining that I shouldn't be this way or know what I know, should just be a regular kid again and not meddle. When I got off, I said, 'Look, see?' and my mom and dad just nodded and looked at each other, like they were afraid. 'I won't fix anything again,' I promised. They are so weird. Is there any more Jell-O?"

She shook her head, careful not to upset the candies.

The boy sat on the armrest with his knees folded up. His face prickled with heat. He picked his nose and stared through the window. Adult lives spread out before him like big sloppy maps their owners could not refold. He leaned over Grace's head and waved bye-bye.

She felt the breeze on her face and was sure they were moving, with the boy at the helm. Better him than me, she thought. She heard a giggle as they took a wild turn. A cool wind traveled into the rings on her eyes and continued on through her. Nothing was on her mind.

In a whisper, the boy practiced for the next day: "I had a great time last night . . . my mother would have called but she is busy . . . no, *indisposed*. Our needs have changed. We no longer have a need. You'll make a great nanny to some other kid . . . That sounds good. End with that."

DEAD HORSE PRODUCTIONS

As if running through a great headwind, the horse's eyes were squinted, the lips pulled back to show the teeth, the whole head snaked forward and the ears laid flat. The impression of speed and determination in something so hulking and still was disconcerting. So was the untouched hay a few feet off, so much the possession of the horse that it seemed as if the animal might rise simply to fulfill the promise to eat it, the illusion of a dead man's full planner.

It had died in the worst spot, too, perfectly aligned with the kitchen's generous window. It rose up in Bill's peripheral vision as he leafed through the phone book, first in the *H*'s for horse, then in the *D*'s for dead and dig. He looked up and met the dead horse full on for the hundredth time that day; much as he hated seeing it, half-seeing it was worse.

"Hi, my name is Bill and I have a dead horse I need taken care of; could you—"

"Excuse me, sir? Sorry to interrupt, but you should know Dead Horse Productions is an independent film company."

The horse was mother's animal, and he was on his mother's farm, a now-defunct boarding stable she had run for the last twenty years. She had been a forceful, obsessed woman, and the training of horses had consumed her life from the time she was forty on, though she always lamented those lost years before. "If only I had gotten into horses sooner—think of where I'd be now!" she'd say, though to her family her fortieth year seemed her last true appearance. Bill remembered her being an active, curious woman who could have been noted for the light and easy way she picked up and dropped passions. Ice-skating, archery, poetry, music—Marie had tried them all and then let them go in a way that denoted not fickleness, but an admirable attempt to experience as much of the world as possible. Her children, largely raised in the pre-horse years, picked up this trait, and therefore none of them could understand her sudden and complete shift from a faintly amused woman resting lightly on the surface of things to a woman so inextricably joined to her passion that her house was literally grafted to her stable, with back windows that opened to the barn aisle.

Despite all this, he had picked up very little about horse husbandry, and certainly nothing about what to do with their carcasses. He sat cross-legged on the kitchen floor, leafing through horse-care books for any clue and glancing at the clock. He knew he could call Fran, his mother's longtime stable hand and student, but he frankly did not want her involved. Fran had been his mother's riding student for over a decade, and when Marie's health began to fade and her horse boarding business was gradually dismantled, Fran had stayed on, still taking care of the barn in exchange for riding lessons and nominal pay. Fran did not believe Bill's mother was senile, or perhaps she did not believe that senility could touch the exalted core of his mother's horse-wisdom. For Fran, like so many previous riding students, was a loyal acolyte of his mother. Acolyte—there was no other word for it. The zealotry of the horse-world was another part of his mother's new life that baffled him—who would have thought his cheerful, funny mother would one day have followers?

His mother's absence gave the house and adjoining barn the eerie feeling of a holy place newly fled. Everything about her house and stable was deeply ritualized—she rose at a certain hour, fed the horses the same time every day, opened the barn's sliding doors a certain width, hung the halters so all the metal rings were lined up so one could look straight through them and see the wood of the tack room wall beneath. His mother had been unable to perform these tasks in recent months, and when Bill had moved in to both help her and assess her deterioration (he and his sisters had lived with his mother in shifts), he noticed the obsessive care Fran took in upholding these compulsions. Whatever his mother had done, no matter how inessential, Fran did. Fran fed the horses at the same hour, mucked using only the blue fork, never the green, walked out into the pasture and manually slapped the horseflies off the horses for two hours each morning, and wiped her boots twice on the bristle brush, and Bill had noticed that once after he walked out of the barn's sliding door, Fran stole up behind him and slid it open a few inches more—the ordained span.

Now he almost wished Fran were here. If he didn't find a way to get rid of it, the dead horse would be the first thing his mother, his sister, and the nurse would see when they drove down the long, winding driveway; the first sight to spill through the bright kitchen window, the last thing they'd see at night, since the horse was fast becoming a white lump on the otherwise unbroken plane of the pasture and he could only imagine how the moon would light it up. He could picture the scene of fragile dignity as his mother unbent from the car and walked to her home, flanked by a nurse and a daughter. Such a situation was already so delicate—already so sad—that the only way it could be partially redeemed would be if his mother walked to her own front door with a steady and sure step, a kind of physical if not mental lucidity. The dead horse would throw this all off. His mother would see it and swerve, stumbling in the banked snow on the driveway's edge while his sister and the nurse wondered aloud about the "sleeping horse." He could picture his mother looking over her shoulder at the dead horse while the two women led her forward, and that image of his bold and passionate mother being kept from a truth (and knowing it, even through her confusion) struck him as tragic an indignity as anything she had yet endured.

But all this pivoted on the dead horse. He bore down on the phone again. He called excavating companies, animal control, even a crematorium, who assured him that, yes, you could burn the horse but it would take at least four or five hours, and that the incinerated hair on the burning hide would produce an odor that may linger for days. He called a rendering plant operator, who asked thorough questions about the weight, height, horse-shoe size and body fat of the horse, before saying that, yes, he was more than willing to come get the carcass—tomorrow. The excavator explained that no one digs in January, and to get through such a thick crust of frozen soil would take his 670 Bobcat, and the 670 had a cracked block and was sitting outside his window waiting for a clear day for him to load it up and take it to scrap. Animal control, once he got through, helpfully directed him to the places he'd just tried.

He hung up, put on his winter gear, and went out to the pasture to see what could be done. The dead horse's greasy black bubble of an eye opened to the sky, and there was a network of cracks in the pupil, like the thin shattered crust of a partially frozen lake, everything still swimming beneath. He leaned over to see if the hide was frozen to the ground, stumbled, and fell on the animal's bloated barrel. Splayed over the dead horse, he felt a subtle collapse beneath him. He flew backward in a spray of red dots. For a panicked moment he thought that by falling on the horse he had somehow forced the blood out of it. He pictured a red burst out of the hind end like a crushed tube of paint, but then he felt the hot points on his upper lip and realized he had a nosebleed.

He tipped his head back and squeezed the bridge of his nose and tried to make his way toward the barn without stumbling. As he walked blood slid down his upturned cheek and into his left ear. All he could see was the gray-blue cloudless sky and the flakes spiraling like bubbles exhaled from a fish as he glided through the pasture, the tip of his nose the highest point, like a fin. He felt for the barn's side door and swung it open, and in the dark and dankness he was greeted with a chorus of whinnies and celebratory stall-kicks—the survivors expected their dinner. "I don't have anything for you," he said, weaving under the fog of their joined breath. He groped for the old rotary phone on the beam and rubbed around for Fran's phone number, which was carved below. Since he couldn't look down, he had to squat low to read the number and dial over his head. "Fran," he said in a gurgling nasal, "Fran, I need you to come to the house."

"I'll be there," she said, articulating each word, he thought, as if they individually constituted a triumph. He hung up and tested his nose. The moment he lowered his head enough to see in front of him a clot broke loose and the divot above his lip was freshly flooded.

In ten minutes, Fran made her entrance. The tracks of the big floor-to-ceiling rolling door were stopped up with ice, but Fran, with a kick of her toe and a hard pull, threw it open with such force that it hit the stops and wobbled. With the sun spilling from behind her and her arm still flung out with the force of the pull, the gesture seemed meant to cast obliterating light on the hidden and unseemly. "What happened to Huey?!" She demanded so broadly that it seemed she was asking not only him but the horses, cats, and weevils. "Huey?" He drew a blank and then remembered: the horse's name. The idea that the carcass—gruesome bane of his day and threat to his mother—should be referred to as "Huey"! A macabre humor must be at play, he thought, though any name connected to the thing would jar. "It—he—was like that when I looked out the window this morning."

For a moment Fran was quiet. In her dirty Carharts with the lumpy gray-streaked braid down her back, she hardly cut an imperious figure, but she began to subtly draw herself up. She angled her chin up and away and drew in a studied breath: she was the barn's nobility, the decreed conduit to the highest authority. "Your mother," she said, "would want an autopsy." Her hands were lightly folded in front of her, the fuzz on her upper lip still and serene, her tightly lined pucker of a face clenched and certain. "The vet could come and do it right in the pasture." Ah yes, there would be nothing more comforting, no better harbinger of his mother's future, than for her to step out of the car and set her eyes on a split and spilled horse carcass and a vet holding up an organ to the winter sun to check for irregularities. He felt a hot slick on his upper lip and tried to blot it with the back of his hand.

"I don't think so, Fran. The horse is dead, and I don't see any need for the expense and bother of an autopsy. I want the body out of here by the time Mom gets home. That's why I called." As he spoke, Fran moved away and began fussing with a frozen latch on one of the stall doors. She then smacked her pants and walked away without a word, placing her feet down with such exaggerated heel-toe precision that it was clearly the middle-aged-woman version of stomping.

"If you leave, don't bother coming back, Fran." She turned so fast that her thick, ugly braid swung around like a creature's tail wielded in defense. "I'm going to take care of the horse. If you want to move him this afternoon, it's time to get going. Moving a horse isn't a small job." She set out for the pasture and he followed her out but from a distance. They walked out to the dead horse in a perfect line, Bill stepping into Fran's boot steps, the two of them separated by three thousand flakes that fell in the space between them. The dead horse was now white with snow. Its dark eye seemed to generate the only heat, and flakes slid over it, melting on the way down.

It turned out that his mother, prudent horse keeper that she was, always dug a trench just in case a horse died in winter, when the ground was too frozen to dig. All Fran had to do was borrow the Halbright's backhoe, easily done since the Halbrights already owed her and his mother one for taking care of their cows when they were stranded two states away. The idea that his mother had preemptively dug a grave was, given her present condition, inherently troubling, and it was even more so when he actually saw it. The hole was several car-lengths long, narrow, and deeper than seemed necessary—a huge black gap demanding to be filled, like the mouth of a baby bird who gapes so wide it threatens to consume itself backwards. It was so thorough a preparation for the unexpected that it might as well have been an invitation.

Fran soon returned, navigating the machine over the pitted winter pasture. He could see the teal spot of her head wrap and her upright posture in the seat—the bearing of a woman grimly certain of her good works. He drew his hands into his coat sleeves, walked over, and unlocked the gate for her. She maneuvered around, working the gearshift, snaking backward, making a pointless show of her mastery with the machine before dropping the bucket and lifting the dead horse. The head rolled, the icy mane hung straight down in a heavy fringe, and the eyes bobbled in the sockets, like the mugging signal of a silent comic on the cusp of mischief. The dead horse's undignified flopping was blunted by its bigness into a kind of joke, with Fran's hyperseriousness at the controls making her a dour and pitch-perfect straight man.

The bucket tipped. The horse's hooves traced an arc in the winter air as it rolled out. He shut his eyes and waited to hear the deep bass finality of the carcass hitting bottom. *Now it's just a matter of sending her home*, he thought, relieved to have the problem of the horse exchanged for the problem of Fran. But when he opened his eyes, the horse was still there, still frozen in its horizontal gallop-stride, somehow spread flat on the surface of the hole. Fran had jumped down from the machine and was fluttering around the horse, poking and peering. He became more and more impatient, figuring Fran was stalling so she'd still be around when his mother got home.

Finally he walked over and saw the problem. The horse seemed to be stuck on something, but he couldn't clearly see what. He passed his hands between the horse and the edge of the hole. There was nothing. He walked around and did the same with the other side. Nothing— there was no branch or outcropping holding the thing up. Finally, to put an end to this business, he lay on his back in the snow, scooted towards the rim, and hung his head down backwards to see what the horse was snagged on. Since the legs of the dead horse were canted sideways, he could see under the entire body, could see the snow lightly swirling around, could see the unbroken air beneath, could see how the horse's body hung down rounded and full, as if suspended on something yielding. Nothing held it up. For a moment he thought that perhaps this was the way a dead horse behaved during burial; that there was always a little lag before the thing sunk down, a consequence of rigor mortis or the gasses in the earth adjusting for it or something—he glanced at Fran on the far side of the hole and she too seemed to be waiting through a typical stage, her face impassive and expert under her head wrap. She had certainly seen this before.

His immediate reaction was to push down on the horse with his foot. Given the icy conditions, and given that the horse was far enough from the edge that he had to strain a bit to reach it, he very nearly fell when he bounced his foot against the horse and felt nothing, no shift. He then leaned over and pressed the horse downward with his hands. The hide seemed to have bristled up in defense; a few hairs pricked the skin under his fingernails. He had to will himself to really push—the dead horse reminded him of both the fragility and noxious potential of a puffball mushroom; he didn't want to find out what the horse would release if broken through. Still he pushed, with his head turned away and his eyes squinted, and under his hands he felt nothing but the kind of unforced and certain resistance of the ground beneath his feet. The horse hung like the earth itself, held up by stratum upon stratum, tucked in its tight spot of space, orbiting on its track, scaffolded by the universe.

"Get back. That's not how it's done." Fran pushed him aside with as much fervor as if he was standing in the path of danger and his left leg slid out from under him so he was nearly forced into the splits. She bent down and began to massage the horse downwards with the heel of her hands while he looked down at her, at the ratty braid and the tense sure twitching of her back muscles under her winter wear. How could she say that he was doing it wrong? Is there really a *right* way to deal with something like this? What precedence, what protocol? Fran continued to pulse her hands along the parts of the dead horse she could reach with an obvious methodology; she radiated her touches outward then inward with increasing speed. Maybe she knew what she was doing. She must.

But the horse did not move. How typical of Fran, how typical of his mother and Fran, to make something as straightforward as dropping a dead horse into a hole into an ordeal of multiple steps and complications. He had noticed whenever he'd visited and ventured into the barn that the two women would make something simple—say, feeding the horses—into a complex choreography that lasted half the night. His mother would man the wheelbarrow full of grains, powders, and potions, and Fran would hold a plastic bucket while his mother doled out each horse's custom blend—a cup of grain here, a dash of powder there, a squirt of corn oil from a repurposed dish-soap bottle. Then Fran would scuttle off with the bounty and pour it into a stall bucket, scuttle back, and report to his mother the horse's reaction to the concoction, be it ravenous or nibbling, then his mother would nod as if that's what she expected to hear and continue pouring and mixing, often dripping the oil from way high up, like a theatrical bartender, while Fran held the bucket, eyes upturned, as if waiting to be anointed.

There was no need for him to tolerate this hocus-pocus now. "Out of my way." He squatted down next to Fran—who continued to knead the horse like a kitten looking to bed down—and threw his arm in front of her. He heard her sputter as she flew backwards. He had no idea what to do, but he felt a sudden need to show Fran his decisiveness, his fitness for the problem at hand. With a great violent motion he plunged his right elbow into the carcass with his left hand pushing behind it; it was a motion of a ninja, a professional fighter, or at least it felt like it to him. But when he made contact the horse was so unyielding that his elbow stung, the pain vibrating up as if his bones were tuning forks; he felt it in his teeth.

"Huey never did like to be forced into anything," Fran said, her voice edged with an edifying aggression. "Your mother spent three hours once trying to convince him to cross a stream. Once she gave up he leapt across." She smiled faintly as if the horse's levitation was a charmingly typical disobedience, further proof that her read on the horse had all along been correct. She moved past him and resumed her work on the horse with a slick and unconscious certainty, like a pianist experienced enough to let her mind wander. Her deep composure in the face of something so bizarre and unprecedented suddenly so offended him that he wanted to grab her by the shoulders and demand to know how the carcass, stubborn though it may be, managed to upturn all natural law and hang there. It was an insult to both normality and to the miraculous to act as if no line had been crossed, to behave as if nothing amazing was underway.

"You can't rush a horse. She always said a horse knows no clock. There are no clocks in the barn and you'd catch holy hell if you mounted a horse with a watch on. She took a watch off me once and threw it under a horse so I could see what they think of time. I was picking cogs and whatnot from that horse's hooves all afternoon . . ." She spoke as if the watch's destruction was a spiritual turning point.

"Well I for one don't want to wait for a dead horse to decide its time to fall in a hole. It's freezing. What are you trying to do, anyway?"

"It's a special massage your mother created for the horses. You do bodywork on the horse from head to toe. Eventually the horse will relax enough to accept what he is asked. See, you start with the crest of the neck . . ." Fran reached across the empty space and wiggled the highest point of the arch in the horse's neck. Snow shook off and floated to the hole's bottom as if the dead horse was a lower cloud in a staggered atmosphere. She went on to explain the various pressure points, the way this or that spot was connected up with this or that nerve and therefore emotion, and it was clear his mother's teachings were a beacon in even the bleakest most bizarre moments. In fact, Fran seemed to be glad to get to draw upon his mother in this most extreme of cases; it was the same small thrill an emergency physician might feel as a particularly broken patient slides through the doors, a chance to apply an education to the fullest.

He listened to her absurd spiel without a word, watched her work on the horse for a few more moments, then walked over and squatted next to her like a patronizing waiter, false-familiar. "Are you sure you're working his shoulder correctly? I wonder if you're making contact with the right nerve." He wanted nothing more than to break Fran of her nonsensical ideas, her adulation of his mother and her every passing thought, her quiet and steady certainty about things of which no one could be sure. He was being forced to take on the full mystery, terror, intellectual and practical burden of the dead horse, while Fran checked out into a world of New Age horse homeopathy and, of course, his mother. *Isn't that just the way it is*, he thought, *you're stuck with someone who doesn't get it.* The last time he vacationed with his mother, at the beginning of the horses, he had noticed that a rock right in front of them lined up perfectly with a mountain, its contours perfectly mirroring the peak in the distance. See, he had said, see? But she hadn't seen, even after he took her gently by the shoulders and moved her around to the best vantage, even after he had pointed and explained, even during the sunset when both mountain and rock were most crisply defined. I don't see, she said, which sounded to him like a personal philosophy, and her inability to see made the sight itself—that sublime visual joke—a burden to him every moment it went unshared.

"That thing you're doing, that . . . *massage* is never going to work. Why not just push it down with the backhoe?"

A panicked calculus went on behind her eyes. Her mouth opened and shut, and the low sun bounced off her gold crowns so her mouth winked shut a small sun each time she thought better of speaking. The thumb on her right hand tapped the other four fingers over and over as if she was counting in groups of fours. That, *that*, was his mother's definitive tic, and it so invoked her that he could not make sense of the image. It was like flipping on a favorite sitcom and seeing another actor in the key role, speaking and doing everything like the original but with a different body, a different voice, the rest of the cast behaving as if nothing had changed. Fran was not his mother, not at all, but the motion of her hand was; it was a small part of his mother evoked through a tiny gesture, it was a piece of her settled on Fran, stunning proof she had blown apart and scattered wide.

Finally, she spoke. "Marie would want me to try her way before . . . resorting to force." In Fran's halting tone there was nothing of her businesslike bravado. She was afraid of trying the backhoe. Afraid it wouldn't work—because if the full force of the machine bore down on the carcass and nothing happened, the floating horse would have moved into a more certain plane of paranormal. Afraid it would work—and his mother and her massage would have been bypassed, overthrown, disregarded, unneeded, unheeded—it would be, for Fran, a death of a god. No, the backhoe would not do. The dead horse was no doubt a mystery, no doubt a problem, but there were many mysteries and many problems, and if you had to forsake something to solve each one you'd have nothing left for your trouble. "Nothing left to do but finish the massage." Fran summed up, her voice stronger now.

Bill did not agree. He would give anything to see the damn thing drop, to feel the ground shake as it took on its weight, to hear the hooves crumple and hit the ground with the reflective, dangerous sound of two like weights striking—hoof and ice equally matched, hitting like the heads of two hammers. The dead horse was a mystery, to be sure, but it was a mystery that had overstayed its welcome. There had been mysteries and inexplicable things throughout his life— strange forms in the trees on summer camp nights, flashes of light in the dark, lost things, such as keys, turning up after years of hiding, things lost (things you *just saw*) and never found, his mother's late love for horses, his mother now. One could learn to live with these mysteries, but a floating dead horse, in all its corporeal fact, could not be endured. Once the horse fell, he was sure he could find an explanation, some liberal reading of science or physics that would diffuse the mystery just enough so the edges blurred and the dead horse, like the other mysteries, would recede into a kind of fog, a harmless atmospheric, which, strange as it was, he could still walk through.

Fran had begun to whistle as she worked, and it was this ludicrous sound that finally drove him to it. He sprinted toward the backhoe and jumped up into the cab and tried to put the thing in gear. He had never used any heavy machinery, and the dashboard, if it could be called that, confused him. He moved a lever up and down, the machine ran roughly, and the bucket, which had frozen to the ground, rose up with a high, shattering crackle, like a prehistoric mastodon waking from a fossilized slumber, shaking its tusks free first. The response of the machine frightened him; he had no idea how to control or direct what was happening, but he was beyond turning back. The backhoe began to rumble and swerve forward, the wheels jerking right and left, Bill hunched over the controls as if he'd just taken a sudden blow to the gut. The tires spun and threw up snow and ice; out of the corner of his eye he saw Fran approaching with her hand in front of her face, trying to block the spray. He gave it more gas, tried to move the bucket down toward the horse, but it raised to its fullest height, like a hand lifted in heavenly praise or wound up to strike. He heard Fran's shouts, saw her leaping at the cab like some desperate mutt, and the bucket came partly down but he could see it would not reach the horse, not yet. He accelerated yet again, and this time the machine found purchase and lurched forward and before he could react it was over the edge.

The front tires hung over and spun. The bucket rested on the horse, which had rotated under the pressure so now its back legs hung down straight like a cat twisting in midair to land on its feet. He threw the machine in reverse, and every time he laid off the gas even for a moment, the backhoe rocked forward and threatened to tip. The back wheels dug deeper into the icy sub-layer of the winter pasture and began to lose ground. He rose up off the seat, turned backward as if the machine might follow, and stood on the accelerator with both feet. He could see his mother's house and stable in the distance, could see the clear empty sky and the slight winter breeze shaking up a few frozen branches so they rattled like wet bone. Nothing he saw admitted of the chaos of which he was part. Even the rev of the engine and tires was a thick insulating lull, nothing sharp or panicked, except for a higher whine, a building screech. He spun back around—was the engine burning up? Then he saw Fran standing immediately below him, her head wrap popped off her wide-strung ears. She was yelling at him. He saw her mouth move. At first he did not hear her, but the repeated rhythm of her cry finally got through: *Turn it off, turn it off!* He couldn't run the thing hard in reverse forever, so he turned it off and readied himself to leap off as it fell. But the backhoe simply swayed a bit as it quieted, and the rush of adrenalin abandoned him so he sat, stunned and stupid, while Fran called his name.

He finally climbed off the machine. Fran was quiet as she watched him descend. Her brown-gray hair was dotted with dry felled snow, as if her head was sprouting small white blooms down the length of dropping stems. Her mouth, so thin-lipped that it seemed a fissure in her face, blossomed outward, quivering and wet. She put a fist, clad in a thick winter glove, up to her mouth and sank to the ground, her back against the machine, the snow piling on her bare, bent neck. Her sobs were so quiet they could have been the tiny pings of snowy sleet on the backhoe, could have been a laugh three properties away carried in and altered by the winter wind.

His mother's house and stables, the fence line, Fran, the driveway—these images seemed to bulge with an aggressive particularity, it was as if the dead horse was an accent mark, changing the emphasis and making everything foreign. He looked up at the falling snow, so hushed and composed, and felt a sudden vertigo, as if the snowflakes were actually still and he was slowly levitating upward, giving the illusion of their fall. He sat down. A red drop from his reactivated bloody nose hit the snow like a burst of fireworks on a horizontal sky. After a moment, he pulled himself along the icy ground so that he was sitting next to Fran. Her profile was slack, her face collapsing into her chin, which receded into her neck, as if her whole head had originally been nothing more than a feat of complex origami, a series of flat folds popped out to resemble a face.

Fran was unmoored, and he was afraid. He thought of something that had happened with his mother. Right after his father moved out, while his mother sifted through her hobbies for some distraction, an orange tabby cat appeared, wormy and starved. His mother had been convinced it was their long-missing cat Sorbet, and she took the cat's return as a reversal in her fortunes. *See, you lose one thing and something else comes back*, she'd say, doting on the cat with a pleasure he had not seen since the split. But the cat was obviously not Sorbet, who had left eight years prior and was two shades darker, and he laid out the evidence to his mother. She replied *I knew it* and sunk down and in as if being drawn through a straw at her feet. What had troubled him most, he recalled, was not the impression that his mom had indeed known and permitted herself to believe otherwise. What most disturbed him was how easily she gave in, and the haunting tone of self-reproach as she shooed the cat away.

He stood up in front of Fran and lifted his hands in the air several times in front of her as if trying to whip up the wind to pull her to her feet. She rolled her head toward him with a heavy looseness; regarding him and the icy pasture beyond with the sardonic gaze of someone who had been awoken from a deep sleep by the tail end of a bad joke. There was a lethargy in that look, a somnolent dark wisdom that seemed to echo the dead horse in that it was both disturbed and irrevocably in repose. He did not let himself be stalled. "*Fran*," he said, bouncing a bit on the balls of his freezing feet, "I think the massage might work. It probably was working before I interrupted." He swung his head back toward the hole where the curve of the horse's hindquarter still peeked above the edge, a half-moon of hide arched like a doubting brow.

"I bet you just didn't do it long enough. Or maybe you forgot a step. Didn't my mother have another step in the massage?" He gestured frenetically over her; he mimed a more perfect massage. His face flushed with impatience and a building panic; restoring Fran seemed the keystone to getting free of this bizarre business. He thought again of his mother making that trek from the car to the house, nurse and daughter guiding her every step, and it seemed essential that Fran, at least, still saw a powerful sage, a spellbinder. "Maybe you missed a pressure point, or maybe you started at the wrong place." Fran's hooded flinty eye rolled either in dismissal or in a circular assessment of the scene: snowy ground, house and stable, his stricken face, the backhoe bucket-edge, the horse just out of sight.

He squatted down in front of her and began to rattle off all the ways she might have mishandled the massage in a ragged low whisper. Though she remained silent, he kept repeating himself, like a refrain, but soon even that disintegrated into a wandering monologue about how his mother must always be trusted in these cases, though this case had never, should never, and possibly was not occurring. The idea that a dead horse floated a mere ten feet away made everything he said seem, at turns, superfluous or courageous—what could he say in the face of such a cosmic aberration, and listen to how boldly he spoke despite the aberration. Fran's eyes had the buffed sheen of faraway thoughts, and she gave him a pitying look, as if he was the one operating under a harmless, but poignant, delusion. That look—though perhaps he had misread it—frightened him more than the dead horse itself. It seemed to indicate this grand shake-up in the world's logic was just another disappointing fact of reality to be faced, another test of one's maturity, one's grace.

"Think about it—you must have missed a step."

He walked back to the hole, kneeled, and saw what they had

missed. Under the dead horse, an ice shelf zigzagged, leaving parts to dangle down, a photo-negative of a darting ice crack, a rent in the loose open air expressed as substance. The horse's tail fanned upon it. He was sure it had not been there before, he could not be sure it was there now.

"You just tell me what to do," he said, his hands already on the horse.

KEY PHRASES

I had to fire Mol. Today was the day. The regional director had called me and told me, apologetically, that they had received enough complaints about Mol over the last six months to necessitate it, and that the previous person in my position had issued her several warnings, none of which had made any difference. "I'm sorry you have to be the one to do it so early in your employment," he had said, "but at least you don't know her too well yet. That should make it easier." He was right; I did not know Mol at all. She was simply an unkempt and increasingly occasional presence in the office next door.

I'd been working for Journey's End Memorials for only two months when I heard from the director. Our company made videos of deceased loved ones to play at funerals or wakes, but I was assured, during my interview, that the workplace was nonetheless "youthful and upbeat." To demonstrate, I was invited to a family fun picnic by the upper management the first weekend after I started. I'd been to enough company fun days in my working life to know this could be a cheerful drunken group-vent or a snake pit of office politics, where every ketchup pass represented a subversive uprising or an affirmation of an inexorable power dynamic. But the picnic was, instead, a desperate counterbalance to what I would discover was as morose a workplace as it sounded. The paper plates were cut to resemble gravestones, and different managers roasted each other by delivering mock eulogies; the speaker with a beer in hand and the roastee standing on a picnic table, a bedraggled funeral wreath about his neck.

During this display of forced gallows humor and impenetrable inside jokes ("Paint the dove, Georgie. Paint it!"), a youngish woman, laughing and splotched-faced, stopped to say hello. "Isn't this a riot," she said, as she unwound a piece of corn silk from her teeth with her pinky nail. In truth I found the proceedings disheartening—I was hoping Journey's End might feel different from my old job, more real and involving. I had just left a job managing a team of secret shoppers, a group of six men and women who practiced being invisible, the kind of customers a business would mistreat with impunity, since their personhood seemed in question. As I coached them on how to be ever more unobtrusive (while still making enough demands to put the supermarket or whatever through its paces), they would move down the scale of presence—from coworkers, to strangers, to movie extras milling in the frame, to flat images, to simply thoughts. Even when I had their attention, I found myself tapping shoulders and grazing forearms to confirm all of us were there. I hoped to get away from that.

The woman began glossing the jokes and references. "You see, George once dumped a live dove in a bucket of food dye, since he needed a clip of a cardinal flying . . ." She asked me where I was from (downstate), if my family liked it here (I lived alone), and then she asked how that was working out, and it was here that I began heeding the training from my former job. I let my eyes focus on a middle distance, past her face but short of the snorting, bald manager wearing the wreath like a puffed-up Cesar. I hunched my shoulders slightly, and pulled my arms inward, compressing my physical presence. When I told her living alone was fine, my preference really, I flattened my slightly eastern dialect into that of a bland midwestern, midcentury broadcaster.

It was only when I let my thoughts stray to my new apartment (alert distraction is what we'd called it, think of something else but still pay attention to when and how you're served) that the woman herself began to disappear. The heavily furnished rental, full of antiques and personal baubles from the owner, made me feel like an intruder, and I was careful not to take up too much space, sitting on only one of the easy chairs and never opening the second bedroom closet. This woman was like all that musty furniture—oppressive while ostensibly offering hospitality and comfort. That was my first, and longest, interaction with Mol before I was told to fire her.

I was hoping to leave a message on her voicemail, rather than having to do it in person, but Mol had inexplicably shown up at work, dressed sharply and full of heretofore unseen passion and competence for the job. All day I heard her answering and making calls in a crisp and comforting tone—a must in the business of memorial videography. All of us were supposed to use a list of euphemisms for death, funerals, and the bereaved, but few of the workers I oversaw bothered. Yet all day I could hear Mol using the key phrases: "memorial gatherings," "remembrance festivals," and "celebrators." I even heard her refer to funeral-goers as "loving reminiscers"—her own inspired creation.

But Mol was terribly unreliable and had seemed, in the few exchanges I had had with her, to not even register what she was doing wrong. "Mol," I had said to her, "you've come in late for the last three days. Do you want to tell me about that?" We were in my office, which I had taken over from someone who had papered the walls in complimentary notes from happy customers. Many of the notes were written in the same hand; I suspected he had written at least a quarter of them himself. "You really made Harry's passing a wonderful memory in and of itself," I read over Mol's head as she replied. "Have you ever just had one of those days when you feel like you're still living in the previous day and you have to spend half the day convincing yourself that there is a noticeable enough difference between yesterday and today to warrant going through it?"

Mol was clearly a clueless woman, but from what I understood she needed the job and expected to keep it. It fell to me to revise this belief. Like anyone, I stalled. I found work that I convinced myself was more pressing; I watered all the plants in the office, de-headed all the dead flowers, shuffled papers, then steeled myself to do it. I saw Mol bent down at the copy machine, her curls shiny from some kind of spritz, the back of her pumps slipping off her heel as she crouched and spun a knob to dislodge a paper jam. Introducing a dramatic new element—the sadness, questions, and finality of her firing—into the blandness of a workday struck me as needlessly disjunctive.

"Mol," I began, and she turned to face me with a torn piece of copy paper in her fist. "I wanted to ask . . ." Her face—unawares, guileless, scrubbed—stopped me up short. "How has it been going with the Halson account?" Halson was a particularly difficult client who seemed to have an endless string of aged, distinguished relatives, one of whom seemed to die each year. His dead relatives were invariably sour-faced and sickly in all the source materials he provided us, yet he expected us to conjure up a video program that showed them as hearty, hale, and good-natured. In all the pictures and home videos he left us, the most recent loss, Great Aunt Halson (a "deeply respected cartographer") had been mostly slumped in a wheelchair or bedridden. In every image, the corners of her mouth were pulled down by deep ruts, and her forehead was wrinkled in an expression of affronted confusion, as if blaming the viewer for her befuddlement. Mapping evidently had taken a hard toll.

"It's going good," Mol replied, straightening her skirt and smiling. "I found this one video of the aunt being lifted from her wheelchair and lowered into a carriage ride in Central Park." The collar of Mol's white button-down shirt was yellowed like the soiled cloud a head makes after years on the same pillowcase. Her skirt, which looked so sharp when I glanced at it earlier, had a broken side-zipper, which Mol had remedied using a row of small gold safely pins. "Sounds great. Like a wonderful moment with the grand old dame seeing the city." I was enthusiastic out of guilt; I saw nothing praiseworthy in her find. Mol gave me curious look, then went on to say that during the moment the aunt was being lowered onto the carriage seat, she had winced broadly in pain. That wince, Mol continued, looked a bit like a smile when spliced against taking-off doves and crashing waves, common motifs we used to transition from scene to scene. "It really looks like a real smile," Mol insisted. "Halson will be so happy."

As Mol jabbered on about the Halson video, explaining how she planned to integrate a map graphic to represent life's journey and kept absently crumpling and flattening out the paper in her hand, I could feel a tightening in my throat. I began to yawn, like I always did when nervous. Once, twice, three times in a row. Mol looked up at me and crinkled her eyes, sucked on her lower lip. "It's not too much, is it?" I shook my head and Mol kept talking. She had a thready bit of lunch around her left incisor. Her right eyelid drooped. The part in her hair was askew. She looked like somebody who was born to be fired. I gave her a little wave with my fingers and excused myself.

I walked toward my office, pausing every few steps with the idea of turning back and giving her the news in mind. I was transfixed by the sheer idea I was on the cusp of action. Whenever I was young and had a boo-boo, and a Band-Aid had been in place for, say, a week, and it was time to let the wound breathe (as Ma would say), I would sit and stare at it, readying myself to remove it. My breath would get short. "At the count of three, I'm going to do it," I would say and then become dizzy with adrenalin as I watched my own hand sitting inert. Moments of truth, as I considered them back then, came and went. It had nothing to do with being afraid of the pain. It was the thrill of knowing that with a single jerk of my wrist I would go from the condition of being deeply Band-Aided to irrevocably without. That was what held me in thrall. Then my mother would invariably walk by. "Wake up, kid." Still walking, she'd snag the Band Aid and rip it off mid-stride. "Go outside and play already."

I hovered around for a while, trying to work up the courage to ask Mol to see me in my office, but then I decided to change tactics. Better to leave a note for Mol and let her approach *me*, rather than seeking her out. That way, I would be ready, and she would be ready. I headed toward her office, which was at the end of a long hallway that very slightly narrowed the closer I got. It was like being drawn down a chute. I had pointed this out to the building manager, who said it was an optical illusion from the old wood paneling warping, but I didn't believe him. Her office was open. I stepped in and shut the door behind me.

Her office was a mess. The desk was covered with papers, some of which looked as if they had been used to clean up a spill. There were flowers everywhere and in everything—some fresh, some dry as old boutonnieres, some thickening into a soup after being left in water too long. She must have collected them from the various funerals she had been assigned to attend. They were in every kind of container— coffee cups, cereal bowls, single flowers in pen shafts with the ink pulled out, a few clipped blossoms floating in an open eyeglass case. Gladiolus spears with their blooms long gone collected thirty deep in one corner, knobbed and curling like a stand of spines. Clouds of fruit flies cycled around the more rotted specimens. A file drawer that was specifically required to be locked was open, and the files were covered with dry, shredded petals and dropped flies. I sifted through Mol's papers for a scrap to write her a note on. Among her papers were reprimands from the former boss, complete with comments Mol wrote in to amuse herself—Windbag, baloney!, over my dead bod, schlub—up and down the margins of perfectly reasonable requests to show up to work and keep company property unharmed. I found a clean sheet: *Come see me at your earliest convenience.—H.F.* I figured I should add something sterner to foreshadow the news that was coming her way. *Please clean out all dead florals from your office, as they constitute a fire risk.* I seemed unable to strike an authoritative enough tone so I added *by 5:00 p.m. tonight.* Then, to soften it, I added that it was because the fire marshall was coming to inspect the property tomorrow in the a.m., though this was untrue. I stood the note up in the keys of her computer and went back up the widening hallway to my office.

I started when Mol knocked even though I was expecting it. I closed the door and asked her to sit down. Though she usually shambled around the office in a casual, tripping manner and threw herself down so loud the springs could be heard in my office, this time she smoothed her skirt and lowered herself primly into the chair.

"I'd like you tell me about how you think your job has been going these past few weeks." I cleared my throat in an officious way as I cast around for how to proceed. "I think I need to hear about how you're perceiving your role here. I know you've missed quite a few days . . ."

Mol leaned forward in her chair and cracked her knuckles. She looked at the ceiling and blew a breath out of her undershot jaw and up her face, causing her bangs to momentarily hover. "The thing is I've . . ." A floating network of her frizzed hair fell between us like a scrim. "I've had a death in the family."

I had prepared for every possible excuse but this. Despite my considerable training in addressing the bereaved, I found myself stammering, full of guilt over my readiness to fire her even though a recent death in the family no way explained the months of unexplained absences and spotty performance.

"I'm . . . so sorry. I had no idea. I mean, you were working so well earlier . . . if I had known. Who—who was it? I mean, if you don't mind me asking."

"It was my great uncle. Just a few days ago, in fact. We were really close. It was totally unexpected. There he was and then—*poof*—he's gone."

Mol put down her head and her shoulders shook. I looked around the office as if for some clue as to how to react. I knew I should go to her and comfort her in a way befitting of my expertise, but the dynamic had shifted so quickly from resolute boss and about-to-be-fired worker to a sheepish boss and grieving worker that I was utterly thrown. I eventually walked over to her and patted her shoulder.

"These are some of the most intense moments in a life," I began, falling back on stock phrases out of my repertoire. "Nothing can prepare us for it."

Mol's shoulder jerked up and down under my hand. She sniffed and made gargling sounds. I wanted to move my hand away from her shoulder, but I realized I would have to say something at the moment I moved my hand to somehow wrap up the encounter, and I had no idea what to say. I obviously couldn't fire her at this moment—that would be cruel. The reprieve was honestly a relief, but I had to still fire her. Her great-uncle dying made her no better worker. The other staff had begun to murmur about who would get her computer, office chair, and shelving—the inevitable was in motion.

I couldn't bear to look down at her, so my eyes were fixed on the clock on the opposite wall, which was in battery-dying indecision: the second hand ticking between the same two seconds. Mol's blubbering petered out with nerve-wracking gradualness, like a roulette wheel ticking to the next number every time it seemed to have stopped. My palm was sweating to the point that I worried it could be felt through her shirt. I pulled away and wiped it discretely on my pants and walked back behind my desk.

"Mol, I think you should take the rest of the day off and regroup." The thought was I could then call her and ask her not to come back. She looked up at me with a sort of wincing panic with one eye half shut as if expecting a blow.

"I want to work. I want to make up for the days I missed. It will help me get my mind off things . . ."

"If you think you can handle it, that's fine. However—" I had to somehow regain my footing. "You need to clean those flowers out ASAP."

Mol looked up and met my eyes with an unnerving steadiness. She rose from her chair and took a low crouching step toward me, as if I were a wild woodland animal, easily startled. She stopped in front of my desk, lifted her right arm, and drew the whole length of her sleeve across her eyes. When she pulled her arm away, a black streak of mascara linked her eyes duct-to-duct, giving the impression that she was peering down at me through a tiny pair of opera glasses.

"I've been saving those flowers ever since my uncle got sick," Mol said, her voice steadying each word so the last phrase sounded so certain as to be a challenge. At the mention of the uncle I let out a syllable of understanding, even though I saw nothing reasonable about saving flowers from strangers' funerals for an ailing relative. "And I've been spritzing them with water. So no worries." She smiled in a poignant sunbeam-through-the-storm manner and tapped my desk with her forefinger as if her next point warranted special emphasis. "Nothing wet can burn."

I began to protest but cut myself off with a grunt that probably sounded like a concession. There was no way to exert power over her at this moment without seeming brutish. I would simply wait until later in the day for her to recover, bring her into my office, and fire her then. These few hours would be a magnanimous offering on my part, a mercy, really, and there was no need to dilute that by harping on the flowers. Let her enjoy her flowers for her last few moments, I rationalized, as I repeated my condolences and saw her out with the requisite pat on the back.

The rest of my day would be busy, and there would thankfully be few opportunities to interact with Mol until I had to call her back into the office for our final conversation, which I mentally slated for four p.m. I spent the rest of the morning in the editing room, watching rough cuts of videos and jotting my comments down on the evaluation forms. *Good work, trim down family's narration, adjust color palette—subject looks sallow in last frame, music too dirge-like, work on youth-to-adult transition.* Mol's video was last in the bunch. She had made the unfortunate choice of overlaying an image of a map over Great Aunt Halson's face so that the roads and streams lay precisely on her deep frown lines, creating a moment where her wrinkles were made monumental and grotesque before her face receded and the video ended on the map alone. *Needs to be reworked*, I wrote for whoever would take over her caseload.

By early afternoon I was back in my office, waiting for a consultation with a new client, when I caught sight of Mol walking down the hall and heard the drag-flop of her loose pumps. Her skirt was twisted tight across her hips, and her pantyhose sagged at her ankles. Right before she turned into her office, we were close enough to meet one another's eyes, and I saw her smile and part her lips as if readying for my inevitable greeting. But I quickly looked down and began shuffling files until she was safely out of sight. I could hear her in her office—the squeak of her chair as she threw herself down, the sound of her typing, which was so aggressive that it seemed she was rolling her fist over all the keys, the crunch-suck as she ate her chips and cleaned up her fingers afterward, even her flower-spritzing. She existed here at this moment only because of what I did not say. By all rights, she should be shoving her flowers in Xerox boxes, yanking the phone from the wall, sifting through her papers, calling HR, making the back-and-forth downcast trek from office to car trunk. I had the absurd sense that I was responsible for not just her continued presence at the job but her existence itself. Every sound I heard from Mol's office seemed to originate with me.

I saw Mol only in my peripheral vision for the next few hours—the hovering blur of her skirt appearing like the spots that swim in your eyes after a glimpse at the sun. Her immanent removal gave her presence a kind of flickering unreality, as if she were an embodied memory of her working self, haunting her old routines. When I saw the dark blip of the back of her head in the viewing room, I almost convinced myself that she wasn't there, that the hazy shadow orb of her hair was simply a halo caused by my astigmatism and the weak light. I foolishly wandered in, and when she turned to greet me I was so startled I jumped and stumbled into a multimedia cart loaded up with editing equipment. Several objects slid off. "Did I spook you?" Mol called cheerily as she walked over and bent down to grope around the dark floor to find what had fallen. Crouched and lit only by the shifting blue light of the screen, she seemed completely altered to me, a posthumous being.

At four p.m., I walked over to Mol's office with the idea of asking her to come see me, but when I got there she ushered me in. "What can I do you for?" she asked as she picked up an old plastic chair, dumped the petals from it, and patted it to invite me to sit. I obliged, thinking that she might be more comfortable hearing the news in her own office among the comfort of her flowers. Since morning, there seemed to be more of them. Sprigs of baby's breath were tucked in the inner wheels of old master tapes on a bottom shelf, and a row of minuscule pink blooms floated in the open trough of an empty stapler. Behind Mol's desk, a sunflower bowed under the weight of its enormous face, the great frilled void looking servile. I ran my hands over the sides of the chair, and when I pulled them away they were covered with apricot-colored dust: pollen.

"Look, before you say anything I want you to know how sorry I am for missing work. Things with my uncle were crazy." A petal on the floor was caught between the crosswind coming from the hall and the upwind from the vent; it swung up, dove, tried to settle, and was shot up again.

"I mean, he was sick for a long time and I was taking him to his appointments and a lot of times I didn't know about his appointments until it was really late so I wouldn't call work but that's what was going on."

Instead of looking Mol in the eye, I watched a vertical crease of flesh on her cheek by her ear deepen and jerk flat with the movement of her jaw. It went loose and tight, like someone playing with the lash of a whip, pulling it so it snapped flat as a kind of threat. A shaft of midday sun barred us from each other; the sun lit each particle of pollen and petal so that it appeared a sparkling densely textured wall had fallen between us.

"I mean, I realize I should have called work. I should have come in.

But I was always so spent after Uncle's appointments that I couldn't call, or even think of calling. I mean, when you're dealing with life and death stuff everything else just fades back . . . in a way it seemed disrespectful to call work when my uncle was heaving on a hospital bed, I mean, he would have given anything to be energetic enough to have a job to be truant *from*. I thought it was sort of rubbing it in his face to reach over his body, grab the hospital phone, dial his number and say 'sorry I missed work,' when here's a guy who would give anything to have the life of work and missing work back in his universe. Instead it's meds and missing meds, it's white cell count missing white cells, antibodies and no antibodies . . . I just couldn't call . . ."

Mol was running her hands through her bouquets as if through a lover's hair. Up and down, from bloom to vase, she rubbed. She tried to catch my eye but I was still looking off a bit, unable to meet her glance. The firing—the *inevitability* of it—it seemed something apart from me or my actions, something that hung above us, something that so altered the scene between us that I no longer knew how to think or act; and indeed, thinking and acting seemed beside the point when there was only a single possible outcome. By the time I stood up she would be fired; it seemed a future apart from me. Mol went on.

"Every time I missed work I would be thinking about it so much it was almost like being more at work than actually being there, you know? I'd be thinking of Halson's videos, of just how to cut it when my uncle would be ringing his bell for water or pills or morphine . . . and I'd be so distracted I'd bring him the wrong thing or what he wasn't supposed to eat on a tray and he'd flip the tray when I put it in his lap, and I'd be squeezing peas in between paper towel bent over and I'd be so angry but also relieved he had the energy to be so angry and I'd be thinking, you know what, it's just this kind of thing I could use in a video at work. That spirited moment in a life. I kept thinking that I was really developing as a memorial videographer right then even though I couldn't be at work. So it was like job training, so to speak."

I nodded as if I were hearing her out. I kept thinking that I was about to change her life with the crushing finality of the news. That these few moments of rambling in her office would be the last few moments she was an employee, and the last few moments that the firing from this job would not be a part of her life story. I thought of something a client once told me about having to break the news of someone's death. I don't remember who he had to tell, or what his relationship was to the deceased, but he told me how he went to the woman's house to tell her the news and caught sight of her through the window. She was doing dishes, and he told me he stood there watching her, thinking that this was the last time she was to do the dishes without the knowledge of the death, that from then on all her dishwashing would be informed by the loss, and that he should let her wash and dry each dish before he told her. So he stood outside the window watching her, and it turns out this was a really big load of dishes she was hand washing, and he ended up having to stand there for nearly an hour as she soaked, scrubbed, dried, and stacked. But he relished every minute, he said, because he knew he was watching a version of her soon to be extinct.

I could smell Mol's sweat—I thought I could—it was the smell of a stove burner turned on in a abandoned house, the decades-old dinners coming back in smoke. Or it was the reek of the soupy stems, too long left in water, brought out by the humidity of her speech. She kept talking, and the uncle's illness became a kaleidoscope of details that shifted every which way but into a coherent picture. She was beginning to lose it; I could feel her watching me, trying to gauge if I bought what she was saying, trying to see if she should abandon this strategy or keep it up. Under her desk, her left foot wormed out of her high heel and set about trying to pull her right shoe off, as if her two feet were trying to free each other and make a run for it. She was in her last throes of trying to convince me. She knew what was to come.

I kept my eyes at her feet to avoid her face. I remembered a time I caught a mouse for my mother when my dad wasn't home. She had seen it dart from under the stove to behind the laundry basket and had shoved a clear glass bowl at me with a "Hurry go get it!" I ran over, ready to play the hero, and after a chase and a cornering I brought the bowl down. For a moment I was exhilarated. Then I saw the mouse. It was zipping back and forth in the confines of the bowl, running up the sides and falling on its back, jumping and hitting the top and smacking back to the floor, stunned. Finally it stood still, simply whipping its head back and forth so fast it was almost a blur. It was a seizure, an electric buzz of fear making the mouse almost a mechanical thing, a tripped-up nerve. I let it go. My mother clucked and called me a softy, but it had nothing to do with that. The mouse's fear was so vivid, and so unseemly was its breakdown, that I felt that by being the cause I was somehow implicated in the mouse's desperate, stupid acts. I felt a part of that whipping senseless head.

"I love this job, my uncle loved that I had this job and in fact if I had any footage of him I would pay to have his video made . . . he would be the perfect subject, he was always grinning and laughing, always sitting in a lighted spot so we wouldn't have to even adjust the color."

I coughed, then pretended to cough. I couldn't speak. I had a feeling of being out of body, of hovering above the scene of boss and underperforming worker mid-termination; the situation began to look to me as a diorama of all unavoidable human relations; I could see myself, the small bald dot on the top of my head and Mol, rolling a petal between her thumb and forefinger until it became an oily little talisman from which she would not part. She pressed her fingers down around it and drew in a shuddering sigh, waiting.

The moment was poised, the dead flowers unmoved. I was on the verge of saying something; I felt the heat and pinpricks in my arms, the loss of air. Not a petal fell. I thought of standing, one afternoon, in the checkout line behind my mother, plotting my avoidance of the cashier woman (by ducking behind the cart, pretending to be occupied with the candy display, etc.). No matter what, though, I knew she would say something to me or my mother, something about how cute I was or if I was always such a handful. For whatever reason, this was a great source of stress. But this one afternoon, I suddenly felt a lifting of my worry even as the line thinned ahead. I had the strong feeling that I was not really myself, that my consciousness was unattached to my physical being, and that even as the checkout woman reached over and ruffed up my hair, *I* was not truly the recipient. I felt as if my own self were something that had been arbitrarily assigned to me, and that I needed only recognize this to avoid all discomfort in the world.

ELEGANTLY, IN THE
LEAST NUMBER OF STEPS

Behind a windowed storefront full of live butterflies, Aaron sat at an old Formica table surrounded by numbers. It was night, and the only light in the whole declining strip mall (the sub shop next door was now a check-cashing outfit, the laundromat gutted and for rent) came from his desk lamp. In his mind, the numbers around him were hardly numbers. He had done a lot of thinking about numbers and what they meant, and he had come to the conclusion that no number was valid that did not correspond, exactly, to something in the world. One of his favorite stories about himself as a child, and one that he liked to tell to prove this point, was that up until early second grade he had been taught mathematics using objects such as beans or seeds or marbles. Once he hit second grade, his teacher had made him do a mathematical equation with simply a paper and pen. He had, in his teacher's telling, thrown himself to the ground and demanded beans. Ultimately he had been forced to do the equation without the beans, which was of course easy for him. Still he had glued small beans all over his math homework as an act of protest.

The numbers that surrounded him corresponded to nothing. There was a checkbook with checks torn out from the front, back, and middle, leaving only checks 2442, 2451, and 2485. There were receipts for unknown items. There was a torn box top with a large figure written on it followed by the letters I.O.U. The buttons on the solar calculator they set out for him were worn smooth and the numbers displayed only from their middles up. He held the calculator under the lamplight but still the numbers were no more than curves and lines, like the spine of an old hull revealed by shifting sand. He had brought his own calculator with him, as always, but he still hated when something didn't work. A few times he accidentally tapped an equation into their calculator and smacked the edge of the table when he saw the unreadable result.

This sent the butterflies aflutter. The light of his desk lamp was angled so the butterflies created huge flapping shadows like stingrays on the back wall whenever they moved. There were about fifty butterflies in the net-cage; their purpose was to bring in customers. As he leaned over to examine them his first day, the owner explained:

"These are the ones that aren't fit for flight. See the notch out of the viceroy's wing? That'll make it fly off sideways. See how that painted lady's missing an antenna? That throws them out of whack, too. Castoffs always go in the cage."

Aaron had been working for Final Release for a few years now. The company sold butterfly releases, that is, releasing hundreds of butterflies at pivotal events such as weddings, ribbon-cuttings, funerals. Usually there was some kind of crisis Aaron had to deal with—this morning it had been a complaint about faulty release pods. He had seen one of these botched releases firsthand when the owner went to show him how well they worked. "I don't get what all the complaints are about. These have been rigorously tested," the owner said and pulled the ribbon. The little paper box flattened down and then opened, so the butterfly, a monarch, pinwheeled down to the warehouse floor in the wake of the scale crushed from its wings.

Aaron had offered to redesign the pods, and for a few hours he was in his blissful element. He sat on the concrete floor with a monarch mount, a compass, a calculator, a piece of string, and four stacks of sturdy cardstock in various dimensions. He drew diagrams, he folded and unfolded paper, he slipped the dead monarch in his prototypes, he experimented with the opening mechanism, the amount of force needed to pull the paper envelope apart without the string breaking or the paper ripping. Soon he had a new release-pod design, one that would be safe for the butterflies, cheap to produce, and able to be operated by the frailest hands of their clientele. The owner and his wife were thrilled, but Aaron was not—there was an unsightly crinkle in the way he had ordered the folds, something that wasn't as tight as it could be. He kept refining the way the folds collapsed into each other and had stayed on into the evening to balance the books.

It was late. Some of the butterflies began to roost, stiffly adhered to the sides of the net cage, except for a periodic slow pump of the wings. The effort it took to balance the books left him wide awake; after a moment he reached into the box of crumpled receipts and sale orders and pulled out a scrap. He leaned his head on his hand and began writing out some kind of equation, with square root signs, symbols, numbers, letters, arrows, and circles. Aaron knew exactly where his calculations would lead—they always led to the very same dead end—but there was something meditative in making a fresh attempt.

He worked and worked and finally paused, looking upward. The Birch and Swinnerton-Dyer Conjecture was centered on a long list of variables, in fact, it could best be described as an attempt to play out seemingly infinite possibilities to a fixed end. This kind of math was necessarily so abstract that the theorist needed to create some solid stakes in his mind to keep the whole thing from rising into the ether. "You just need to find your tether," Dr. Bajpai would say, "some system to keep yourself rooted and organized. Because once you wade into a problem . . ." and then he would trail off and gesture to his own system, the strips of crepe paper, covered with numbers, that he hung from the office ceiling. Aaron looked over at the butterflies again. The cage was small, the butterflies flawed and therefore poor fliers, but they were all centers of possibilities, small little suns whose linear rays represented every possible flight, every downward dive their life cycle–end might take.

Pursuing a conjecture had a particular appeal for him. Dr. Bajpai liked to say that the work of a mathematician was not discovery but validation, and therefore the most affirming type of work one could do. The funny thing about conjectures, Aaron thought, was how beautifully simple they were. In fact, they often seemed laughably obvious to anyone familiar with advanced math. But they could not become official theorems until someone did the legwork to show, beyond any doubt, that they were correct in all cases, which meant, Aaron knew, that you needed to find a system to try out all cases. He liked the thoroughness of it, the clever ways one could circumvent a million calculations with a crisp equation, the elegance of condensing reams and reams of numbers and possibilities into a few simple, perfect steps.

Even before he had become interested in math, he had operated with a certain efficiency and directness, a notable lack of superfluity. When first charged with dressing himself, he wanted a faster method than putting on each cumbersome piece at a time, so he clipped his whole outfit together with clothespins (jacket to shirt to pants to socks), suspended it off the ladder of his bunk bed, and jumped in. Routes and paths were of particular importance to him, and every time his mother drove him to school (he could not cope with the bus), he formulated a new route or departure time for her to try, clapping his hands in the back seat and laughing when all the lights were green and his stopwatch read a few seconds less. His father was an inventor of household gadgets who was always streamlining and combining (he invented the kitchen knife with the vacuum handle to pick up the scraps), so he of course approved, while his mother, a Realtor, appreciated having a child who completed his homework and chores so quickly, leaving her free to make calls, bragging all the while that her son could probably close on a house in an hour.

He saw, in all quick and smooth motions (a cat grabbing a bird from the air, a car swerving around a bike swerving around a squirrel, all synchronized, all moving forward) not just efficiency but beauty, but his life thus far had progressed in disappointing fits and starts. In high school he had been clearly talented in math, but his practical gifts caused everyone, including his parents, to push him into business, where his organizational abilities would be of use. During the senior year of his undergraduate degree at Penn State, he had gotten into a car accident that left his upper body in a stiff cast for the better part of a year. The feeling of that cast—the way it restricted him—seemed to hover over him even when it was finally removed, so he still got up from a chair with an extra burst of energy, as if anticipating a debilitating weight. Once he graduated, a year behind, he had gotten a job as assistant head of supply for a kitchen-supply manufacturer, but it was quickly obvious that he wasn't right for the job. He hated the burdensome reporting that accompanied any change he proposed, the roundabout corporate gibberish he was forced to adopt.

After being fired, he floated around, picked up freelance accounting work, played online poker for money; he even visited two county fairs and won, both times, the jelly-beans-in-a-jar counting contest. He moved back home and helped his father test blenders and automated ice-cream scoops, he worked in his mother's garden, he went for walks with his grandparents who lived across town, he applied for jobs in statistical analysis but was turned down. He finally took the job at Final Release, beginning as a butterfly packer but soon taking on their accounting after his boss heard him calculate a complicated return off the top of his head. It was around this time that he became involved with "recreational math," the term used when lay people try to solve age-old mathematical conjectures. He had first been introduced to conjectures in high school, when his math teacher had the class all work on Fermat's Last Theorem before it was solved. When Andrew Wiles discovered the proof in 1995, Aaron had sent away for the journal it was published in and curled up with it for hours as if it were a novel. Just a few months ago he began looking through his old math textbooks for some still-unsolved conjectures and settled on the Birch and Swinnerton-Dyer Conjecture, which concerned itself with rational points on elliptical curves. He began working on it in all his spare time, even mailing what he thought was the proof to the Clay Institute for Mathematics, which offered a prize to whoever solved it. He received this letter back, with his name and specifics in the blanks:

> Dear ——————,
> Thank you for submitting your proof for the ——————— conjecture. Errors appear on page(s) ———————, rendering it invalid.
>
> Professor Abdu Bajpai

This night, like so many others, found him at another impasse with the problem. He made a notation on his paper where he left off, then grabbed his coat and went out the back door for a break. Behind the office, behind the refrigerated shipment van painted with a blue butterfly trailed by hearts, past the shed filled with torn nets, the release-butterflies resided in what was nothing more than a small cement outbuilding with a sliding door latched with a padlock. The whole area was dark. Aaron swung the flashlight back and forth in front of his feet, the store's main set of keys swinging on his belt loop. The arc of the light left a brief trace, sometimes demarking the beginnings of a plateau curve, a parabola, a bicorn.

He unlocked the door and flicked on the light. The room resembled a mausoleum, the walls lined with stacked steel drawers filled with packed boxes of butterflies, all tucked in their little paper wontons for release. The temperature was maintained at forty degrees to keep the butterflies in an inanimate, ready state; nothing moved in the room, nothing could. Aaron pulled open a drawer marked "Viceroy," then selected the sharpest key from the bunch at his hip and pressed it along a length of shipping tape. The flaps sprung open, revealing twenty-four cardboard compartments. In each one, a linen-paper pod inscribed with something—these were inscribed with "Jan & Mike June 23rd"—was wedged in a slit of foam. Aaron lifted a pod out, held it before him, and pulled the string carefully—these were the old, flawed pods. The butterfly did not fly out, but walked out with groggy casualness as if debarking a plane; it made its way down Aaron's arm with its two wings clamped into one dimension. Upon reaching his fingertip it did a slow, labored turn, its legs adhering to one another and tripping it up like the loop of a shoelace.

He watched the butterfly, thinking about an idea that came up in his most recent conversation with Professor Bajpai. After he had received that first form letter, he had continued working, and when he set out on what he considered a radical new approach, he sent a letter detailing it directly to Dr. Bajpai, on a whim. Surprisingly, the professor wrote back to him personally, effusively praising his efforts and pointing out the potential significance of his method. From there, they began a correspondence, first over the mail, then over the phone, and finally Aaron visited his office a few times, lugging a portfolio filled with all his handwritten notes and calculations. The professor seemed to like talking to Aaron, and Aaron liked being able to talk math with anyone. Dr. Bajpai, as old and respected as he was, had an irreverent streak which had at first flummoxed Aaron. Sometimes he ribbed Aaron by pretending not to understand prime numbers and forcing him to explain them, or he would, after hearing Aaron's rapid-fire explanation of a complicated string of algebraic computations, ask in a deadpan voice if A+A+R+Zero+N had any part in what he just said, or if Aaron had been overtaken fully by a mathematical muse. Once he had even answered the phone when Aaron called with a grand announcement that he himself had solved the Birth, Sin-a-Ton, and Die Conjecture, using the pattern of his own life as the primary proof. Aaron used to simply wait it out when Dr. Bajpai got on these tears, but he had recently learned to enjoy them, sometimes even planting amusing mistakes and messages in his work in response.

Aaron bucked his wrist, encouraging the thing to fly off. The creature fell dramatically until it came to, opened its wings, and began flapping inches before it hit the ground. He watched as it flew upward and tapped the buzzing lights, landed on the highest shelf, walked along its edge, then took a long, looping flight back down to the concrete floor, where it pressed its wings together and zipped itself into a single plane.

The butterfly clinches it, Aaron thought in the shorthand of thoughts. Something in the precise delineation of the butterfly's flight—or the way it clenched shut at the end, or the way its wings parted the air, or the way it interacted with the box corner, or its broad relation to all the geometry in the room—something had done it, and Aaron was now as sure as he would ever be that he had the means to prove the conjecture. He bent over the box top and made furious notes, for, as sure as he was, he knew it could still get away; like all great ideas, it manifested itself by zooming by.

He returned to the office and continued working on the problem, startled by the simplicity that now stone-skipped over what he once saw as irrevocable complications. He was calculating so fast he pulled scrap after scrap out of the box, filled it, then tossed it in a box top. The lone desk lamp glowed on his face, his hairline was beginning to sweat, and his thigh was vibrating under the desk, sometimes bouncing high enough to hit the underside and cause his pen to slip. On the wall behind him, the large shadows of the butterflies rioted and undulated as if in a breathless dance-off with his leg. In an hour, he had all but solved it. There were some straightforward calculations left to go, but these were formalities. He was sure he had found the proof.

It was so quiet in the office that he could hear the buzzing of his own head—the faint vibrations of the air over his eardrums, the clicking of breath in his throat. He put his pen down and was completely still for a moment, then looked outside. The whole area was dark but for a strip of light at the warehouse door. He forgot to lock up, again. The last time he did that raccoons pried open the doors and tore into some of the boxes. It was a nasty scene, bits of boxes and butterfly wings all over the floor. He tapped the papers that comprised the proof into a neat stack and went outside. Around him fireflies pulsed in the sky, seeming to Aaron to be fixed points of light flicking on in a vast switchboard.

The door was ajar and he could hear the rustling and scrapes of what sounded like a whole family of raccoons. He pulled the door open and shouted "Get out! Get out of there!" But instead of raccoons, he saw men. They wore low ball caps under dark, hooded sweatshirts. Their blades were stopped in mid air above the shipping tape of a box seam, while crushed boxes and spilled Styrofoam peanuts arrayed around them. Butterflies flapped and flew around the floor like looters in the wake of disaster, while others, broken, spun as they tried to take off on one wing. "Is there anything but bugs in these boxes, fucker? Is there?" The man stood—Aaron could see he was the larger of the two—and moved toward him, waving the knife in front of his face as he approached. A long reddish beard grew down his neck and shot into his shirt like the tail end of a creature diving for cover. "You deaf?"

Aaron stood in the doorway. He assessed the benefits of running, of putting up his hands, of pulling out his wallet and throwing bills; but all of these actions had drawbacks and he was still factoring in the variables when the man was upon him. He curled up and covered his head; his body slid forward and back on the floor as he was kicked; he was a curve, his path was demarking a series of overlapping curves, the boots swung towards him on the axis of the hips in arcs, all this lightly warped, like soft wax, on the curvature of the earth. His face was pressed down by one boot to steady him, as the other kicked his back. "There's nothing but butterflies," he gasped. His left eye felt as if it were spreading flat on the concrete. The view was so low he could see the legs of two butterflies, monumental as the legs of his parents appeared to him when he hid under beds and tables.

"Nothing but dirty fucking bugs; what the fuck . . ." He felt another hard kick to the head as if he were to blame. His vision narrowed and all he could see was a butterfly, a painted lady, moving on its needle legs like a dancer, encircled by a field of black and backlit as if it were the star of the show. "Get his wallet, man, his wallet." They turned him over, held his neck down, then pulled his jacket off from behind; yanked it off like playground boys pulled off the wings of bugs; he would cry and point and tell them to stop until the lunch lady made him take a time out for carrying on. His head hit the metal support of one of the shelves, and a box slid down and settled on the small of his back.

The men ran off. The door was open and a breeze swept through, whipping the butterflies, dead and alive, aloft like fall leaves. Aaron began to curl and uncurl, trying to get the box off his back, convulsing like a worm poked with a stick. The box rolled off and he sat up, lifting his hand to his head, where he felt a stickiness combined with something soft and detached. When he pulled his hand away there was a crushed buttercup wet with blood, only a pinprick of yellow left on its wing. He looked at his hand a long while, then tried to stand. He kicked out his right leg; he tried to push up with his left hand; he stood up with his legs splayed and wobbled before falling to his knees. Another draft came in, and he wanted badly to be outside. The night air would fix it, he thought, *like people going to the sea in the old days to cure things.* He crawled forward, pulling with his elbows, pushing packing material, boxes, and paper release pods in front of him, often stopping and putting his head down. Blood dripped from him and spotted the bits of Styrofoam, creating small red eyes that watched him as he lurched forward again, dragging a sheet of bubble wrap with his toe. He reached the door and with a strong kick tumbled out in a wave of debris. The grass felt so good that he lay for a moment in the healing dirt.

"Right elbow," he told himself, and put it down. "Left foot," and he tried to push off of it, though it slipped back in the dirt. "Left hand," and he reached forward and closed his fist around a clump of grass. "Right leg," and he dug his knee in. He chanted these commands to himself, even when he lay flat, unable to organize himself for a moment. He was afraid; he tried to think of the proof. The proof! He had discovered it. He tried to remember his first attempt. When was it? He put his elbow down. It had been after he had started at Final Release; he had been sitting on the floor in his childhood bedroom, rifling through the bottom drawer of his dresser. He found his high-school math textbook, the one with the picture of thousands of crayons moving down the assembly line on the cover. It contained a very basic description of the Birch and Swinnerton-Dyer Conjecture in a purple sidebar titled "Math Mysteries!" He wrote a few things in margins. The act of writing in a book from his past felt strange. When he looked up his dad was standing in the doorway. "Watch," he'd said, and fired up a turkey carving knife made to look like a tiny chainsaw, complete with a pull.

He slid into unconsciousness like a butterfly sidesteps under a leaf in the rain. Later that week he had begun working on the problem. He thought of how confident he was at first—it looked so simple!—but it had taken all of his concentration. His mother and father were arguing over how to revive a dying shrub outside his window, and their voices kept cutting in. He picked up his notebook and all the loose sheets he had been working on and walked away from the sound. He was looking down, calculating in his head, and before he realized it, he had walked straight into his brother's room, where it was always quiet. It was of course the same—the plaid comforter, the basketball trophies on the shelf, the tennis shoes under the dust ruffle, poking out like two deeply bonneted faces. The room had been vacuumed (how long ago?) and the carpeting groomed in perfect diagonal strokes with curves around the dresser feet.

More time passed. He was again laying down, his forehead rooted in an ant mine. His right hand was knuckle deep in the earth. He blinked, and his eyelashes raked dirt. He raised his head and saw the office door and the ball of pulsing light above it. There was a sound of crickets, a sound that seemed to travel not through the air but through the earth. The sound was like the windup truck that inexplicably began running, deep in his brother's desk drawer, the moment he sat down and put his pen to the problem. The thing had jerked to life among the pens, erasers, and leaves his brother had preserved between bits of paper. The weak grind of the mechanism moving through this detritus had seemed like the room itself waking. He pulled the drawer open and ran his hands among the things; reaching into that dark drawer without seeing what he was touching felt illicit—touching anything in the room did.

The white back door of the office, no more than twenty feet away, rose above the grass like the keystone of some spectral ruin. He breathed in-out-in, counting, as he often did involuntarily whenever he was stressed, but this time the sound of the building numbers in his mind seemed the sole evidence that any time was passing, that any moment trailed a thread from the moment before. His brother's room had been a spacer between two times—the time he was there and the time he was not—and his parents left it untouched as if he might come back and occupy, retroactively, the years he had been gone. Occasionally, they got letters: Drew was in Alaska, hiking with the Inuits! He was in Santa Cruz, selling blown glass vases his friend made. He was bartending in Florida, he was hitchhiking across the plains, he was married, he was separated, he needed cash, he was silent.

He stood, tried to take a step, but his own body seemed infinitely far away, his feet so small that they seemed beyond control, bouncing like electrons, circling the unsteady nucleus of his head. He fell, his vision going in and out so fast it was as if his blackout were on a propeller, spinning in front of his sight. For weeks he had worked on the problem in his brother's room—at his desk—thinking that something about working there was lucky. There was something about the room—the objects so settled in the deep hush, the way even the light seemed to hesitate at the window, casting itself in modest rays that didn't touch anything, didn't even reach the bed—that seemed anticipatory, matching the mood in which he always worked. And he liked touching the things in the room, bumping the shoes with his shoes, running his hands down the duvet cover, opening the closet and clapping the old sport uniforms, Sunday slacks, and sport coats covered in plastic between his hands. He always sat back down to the problem refreshed.

He shut his eyes and relaxed into the earth, which swayed and arched up around him, so at some moments he felt a wall of vertical grass behind his head, sometimes under his chin, and sometimes pressed to his face, damp and gentle as a hot cloth dabbed on his forehead. Afternoons in his brother's room, he would lie on his back on his brother's made bed, imagining the figures and forms of the conjecture playing themselves out on the swirled plaster above. He kept his visits to his brother's room from his parents, only working in there when they were outside or away. He knew that occupying the space would only make Drew's absence more keenly felt, whereas the empty shrine of a room, always shut, was like a brilliant idea waiting to be thought. The ceiling fan revolved but there was no breeze, as if the air in the room were gelatinous, pinching closed the moment the blade passed through. Every now and again a new angle would come to him, and he would reach over to the nightstand and scribble it on the thick block of his brother's neon notepaper. Sometimes he rumpled the duvet when he napped; he drooled on the pillow made to look like a softball. When he left the room for the day, no evidence of him remained. He even made sure the pencils were all pointing the right direction in the pencil holder, the calculations picked from the trash.

Something crawled over his nose. He snatched at his face, sending his head vibrating like the blur of a dog's scratching foot. He pressed his hands over both ears, trying to stop the movement. When he was younger and his brother would get in trouble he would put both hands over his ears and listen to the sound, the ticking and settling of his head, like an old house at night. He honestly didn't remember much about his brother. They were six years apart, and Aaron was twelve when Drew left. All his memories of Drew were memories of trying to remember him. He used to feel guilty about how little he remembered, so he would steal into the empty room, look at his brother's stuff, and half-create, half-recall things that had happened between them, using the objects in the room to star in these inventions. The ant farm in Drew's closet—didn't they mix carpenter and regular ants to see what would happen? Didn't the two colonies burrow from opposite sides, through the sand, so they met and rumbled in the very center while he and Drew made opposing bets on who would win? It was as if the objects held the memories, as if all he had to do was concentrate on a photograph, ball, or toy and an experience he and his brother never had would form, popped like an insect from the amber. Years later he lay in that same room, bearing down on the conjecture so neatly printed out next to him in the bed, waiting for its provenance—the proof—to appear in just that way.

He concentrated on the light above the office door, trying to keep it in his flickering sight. He crawled, lost consciousness, cried out, slithered and kicked, sat up for a few seconds, and fainted. Loose butterflies were tucked in the grass all around like crocus buds. The door was ten feet away. He fluttered his eyes open and saw not the grass, butterflies, light, and fireflies but the thin light under his brother's room's door. "Have you been in Drew's room?" his mother asked, and he had shaken his head without thinking. "The light was on." His father appeared behind her, a jeweler's loop hooked around his forefinger; he was working on something small. The next day they heard from Drew; he was coming home to get back on his feet, or something. His parents pretended to be guarded about it—he had said he was coming home before—but Aaron could sense their excitement. All he thought of was losing the room. He realized the room was just a space, just a weird little place where he worked on a pointless problem—but why should that be upturned? He didn't need the memories of his brother, both actual and invented, diluted by the real thing. His parents left for dinner (a celebratory dinner?), and he lay in Drew's dark room, not venturing the light. He had made great progress towards the proof—the evidence lay spread all around him on Drew's notepaper, on Drew's old homework, even on the back of some girl named Heidi's love letter. He reached for his brother's clear plastic phone, the kind where all the inner workings were lit up and exposed in primary colors.

"You sound a little down," Dr. Bajpai had said. Aaron was surprised. They had never addressed each other outside of math, though math, as Dr. Bajpai made clear, covered a lot of ground. Math could be funny, the professor had pointed out, telling a long joke that played on the ideas of negative and positive numbers, something to do with where to seat whom at a dinner table. Math could be defiant, as when Aaron, when asked to "show his work" in high school, responded by writing up a narrative of the whole development of his mind, from the cradle up until then, to explain how he had come to be able to solve the problem without "work." Math could be mysterious, of course, what with all the conjectures, like the Birch and Swinnterton-Dyer, that behaved as perfect mathematical rules even though they had yet to be proven. But mostly math was oblivious, marching forward in its formations, unspooling into infinity, unimpeded by anything but itself. There was always something you couldn't solve, always a place math could go where you could not, it was like riding a horse in a forest of lower and lower tree branches until you were on your back in the dirt, listening to the numbers gallop off and away. He blinked, opened his eyes, and looked up at the moon. The pinprick stars widened and shook, becoming thin and sloppy before tightening back up into spots.

The door was the door to Drew's room. If he opened it, he would see all Drew's things, the bed, the sports trophies, the pinup in the red suit, the tennis shoes venturing from under the dust ruffle. It was right here in the middle of the lawn. The world tipped and tipped again, and Aaron thought he could hear the objects in Drew's room being scrambled by the motion. Maybe there were butterflies in there now, perched on the trophies, cocoons in the shoes. Fluttering when it was in flux. The sounds made him afraid. What if he didn't make it? Would *his* room, then, become the shrine? Aaron's coat—the one he decided not to take this morning at the last minute—would never move from the old wooden rocking chair in the corner. The math textbook, spine broken, would remain opened to the conjecture, a pen in the slit between pages. His old upper body cast, propped in the corner and signed by all his college friends (mostly his professors, truth be told) would stand sentry like a truncated ghost. The blue pillowcases under his green plaid comforter would become conjecture, known but never again verified. The room would become a placeholder, a zero in the middle of a figure, the absence that anchors the eye when transcribing a long number, the nothing that changes the value completely.

Would Drew tiptoe into his room when his parents were out, running his fingers over the math theory books, the compass for drawing curves, his Final Release work shirt, with the butterfly-heart on the breast? Perhaps he would creep into Aaron's room and ponder some great question, something related to dark matter, what happens when something disappears. Leap up when he heard his parents downstairs and hurry back to his own room, the shoes, the trophies, the red suit . . . As Aaron talked to Dr. Bajpai about his work on the proof, looping and unlooping the phone cord around his fingers, he opened his mouth a few times to confess that yes, he was a bit down, and did Aaron ever mention that he once had a brother? But the proof and Drew were two things he had to reach hard for, grasping this, grasping that, turning from one to reach the other. He lay on Drew's bed, prostrate, trying to bring the threads closed, but Dr. Bajpai, with that warm and wonderful voice, had to go. The lights deep in the plastic phone went off.

He slapped open the door with his forearm and crawled, curve-straight-curve, like a snake, toward the main office. When he was a few feet from the desk, he grabbed the line and pulled the phone off the desk. It was a heavy old mechanical Princess phone, and it chimed in protest as he dragged it towards him. He had two calls to make. He punched the first number with his thumb and began talking the minute he heard a voice. "I've been attacked," he tried to say, but his voice seemed to be dropping vowels and extending consonants, so much so he could hardly understand or decipher for himself what he meant to say. "Need help," he said more simply, and then he mumbled the name of the business and ended with "bu-butterfly" and another help or number or some other SOS sound. Dr. Bajpai, on the other line, was yelling into the phone: "Who is this? What's wrong? Is that you, son? Have you been in a car accident?" Dr. Bajpai kept asking questions, his voice rising even as Aaron passed out, jerking an arm out and flinging the cradle across the floor.

He came to already dialing. It was time to let Dr. Bajpai know. A voice answered, a strange voice, but it was likely Bajpai playing a trick. "I discovered it," he began, utterly lucid, he thought, though the sound that issued from his lip sounded more like a series of underwater bicycle honks. "Sir, can you tell me your name?"

"It's really quite elegant," he went on, then began his brief and careful explanation, answering every question before it could be voiced. "What has happened? Have you been injured? Is anyone there with you?" Ah ah ah, you are not too quick for me, Dr. Bajpai. He laughed and realized he loved it when the old man played dumb. What a wonderful thing that was. "Can you tell me where you are? Please stay on the line, sir, please . . ."

He dropped the receiver, rolled so that his arms spread wide, and waited for what he was sure would come.

A COUNTRY WOMAN

There is a country woman now among us. We can see her from most of our backyards. Whatever you lack she will exemplify in your view—that is, if you are slothful and prone to depression she will be whistling and weeding in the single place in her yard that you can see from the recliner you have not left since last night. If you are needy and rattled when alone you will catch a glimpse of her through her window sitting down with a three-course meal she made for herself. You might even hear the music on her radio—old bluegrass—and hear her sing along. If you are lacking in purpose and passion, you need only see the peppy flick of her muck boots on the sidewalk as she heads out for the day.

"With these two hands and a day's time, I can move a mess of earth," she likes to say, but only to those of us who become impotent thinking of the brevity of days. She is referring to the koi pond she's digging, which she plans to stock with "offspring of her daddy's fish farm salmon," a losing proposition considering salmon's need to migrate, but it seems like a dreamer's envious boldness to those that hear this particular detail. If only they could throw themselves into something so hopeless with such aplomb!

She is at all the parties. To invite her is to send the message: I can face up to my faults. A kind of sweet torture is to engage her in conversation in a corner after having a few glasses of wine. The country woman speaks of many things: her family, the farm, weather changes, ham hocks, apple butter, the orneriness of old roosters as opposed to the sass of old hens . . . None of it means anything to you—why should it?—but the telling is full of charm and homespun wit. Things you clearly lack, if she's displaying them. The only recourse is to keep listening until she loses her charm, thereby affirming yours. It is a convoluted game, and the longer you listen, the more you are entertained and delighted, the more you wince at your own delight, and the more the country woman tries to amuse, sensing your discomfort and trying to alleviate it . . . you end up drunken with your arm around her shoulders, drooling compliments in her ears, as if by foisting your admiration on her you will somehow take on her traits. It is like taking a rubbing of a gravestone with a pencil and paper—the closer you press the better impression it will leave.

It might seem most logical just to avoid her, to keep the shades down and the eye averted, and this we try. One neighbor invests in heavy drapes, tightly locking blinds, and tall wild hedges for her front walkway so she can avoid seeing the country woman in the few steps from the driveway to the front door. And indeed if you walk fast with your head down you need never see the country woman in full. You might hear her whistle as she reams her gutters with a toilet brush or peripherally see the flash of a tartan plaid work shirt through a thicket, but the county woman herself is never again manifest.

Then as sudden as "sow-to-trough" (her saying) she is gone. The flash of her yellow raincoat through the gap in the drapes, the squelch of her Wellington boots, the sound of burning, cooking, nailing, feeding, mucking, whetting, basket braiding, carcass cleaning, pie frying, and meat baking (her order): all this came quietly to an end, as if the country woman had scuttled away in secret though she was the one from whom we hid. We listen for her like the clear tone of a bell long after being struck, a kind of warbling vibration that held us in thrall while we waited for it to cleanly end. Had she gone back to the country? Would she be back? Hers is the most palpable of absences, a not-aroundness so forceful that even her yard, left intact, is ragged, as if something had been rent from it—the pond and roosters and wheelbarrows seem too small for the space they take up, rattling stand-ins for something larger that once fit flush. The neighbors open their windows and beat their drapes with brooms and look around as if relieved but there is a great unease: one could avoid the country woman but not her absence. It was more here than what remained.

LINE OF QUESTIONING

The accused was excited. They walked him down the halls of the police station with the absurd gravity he had expected, but he had not been ready for how intense and real it seemed. My god! The more powerful man—that guy the rookie cop called Sergeant Ron—walked next to him with magisterial bearing, a rolling of the foot in leather boots that was positively, quintessentially, justice performance art. All the details were tuned just so—from the dull green walls to the bored receptionists with the tattooed eyebrows. The halls rang with all their shoes. When they flicked the light on in the interrogation room, the two cops split up, as if the long, white table had cleaved them. The accused sat at the head of the table with a cop on each side, and he had the funny thought that he should say grace, give thanks for this sparkling situation on which he could already feel himself feed. He put his elbows on the table, awaiting their questions.

The alleged victim in this case—raped, bound, left for dead in the brush along the accused's jogging route—was still open on the autopsy table, ten miles from where the accused now sat. That woman—Jillian—was his former student. Ten years earlier she had been in his poetry class. She had sat in the back row and rolled her eyes at nearly everything he said. Her short, red hair was cropped close to her skull and her hair line flamed with acne. One of her ears dripped with jewelry—hoops and turquoise bobbles—while the other was always naked. Sometimes he would fix his eyes on that bare ear while she spoke. She argued with him in workshop in a fast, pushed-out voice, as if there were a gun at her back and she were being made to speak.

Mostly, she defended the worst student poets in the class. If he gently criticized another student's too-easy resolution or tired imagery, Jillian would pipe up in defense. She would claim the bland imagery was refreshingly spare, the facile ending crystalline. Her own work was impenetrable, seeing as it primarily consisted of strings of gerunds, lacking both subjects and objects.

Had he ever seen her on his runs? He had. She always trailed behind a little dog that looked like mop head spread over a football. That dog was found a few days after Jillian went missing—speckled with blood, rooting in a fast food bag—a few blocks from where her body was found. Patches of the dog's fur were then shaved off and put in an evidence bag. Had he ever talked to her? A few times. She had stayed in town after she graduated, and for several years they were in the comfortable habit of looking past one another, an agreed-upon invisibility, since nothing could come of speaking again.

One afternoon he thought he'd spring out of the scenery, out of the backdrop of near-forgotten acquaintances he had no doubt become for her. He imagined she'd look startled or guilty when he spoke to her, but she simply looked bored and moved her lip ring (that was new) around with her tongue from the inside as he spoke. He was sweaty from running but noticed a smell coming off of her, a kind of stems-melting-in-the-flower-vase scent. He ran his hands through his hair, feeling a sudden urge to impress her. "I'm still teaching," he said, which made him sound old, "the students are fabulous. So many promising young poets, so invested in the books I assign, so willing to look to the established forms for guidance yet still so able to genuinely subvert—"

She cut him off. "I renounced poetry. I don't need that falsity in my world. I'm a journalist now." She bent down and rubbed the mutt at her feet. Its small jaws opened and it panted and drooled, sucking at its chops. Later, he researched and found that her "journalism" consisted of a few letters to the editor at the local rag. "Preserving the Dog Park for Living Art's Sake"—a screed about the beauty of running dogs as opposed to the corruption and greed of local lawmakers. "Signage Should Be Azure"—a passionate and rambling plea for the city to lighten the street signs by a shade or two. He printed off these letters and read them while drinking a single-malt scotch. The phrasing had an evocative kind of incoherence that left him wondering if there was some meaning he was missing, some subterranean brilliance that he, with all his background, should be able to pick up. When his glass was drained he threw the letters away and turned to his students' work.

Could he retrace his activities from March fifth? The accused turned a clear eye on the investigators. He knew his should have his "counsel" with him—a lawyer who would hold up a hand and stop him from speaking. Counsel was like the muse, a quietly authoritative presence that slowed and directed the flow of expression. The accused thought of his own work. The muse had not been with him lately, maybe never. He still churned out books of poems with lovely matte covers and abstract cover splashings at regular intervals. Lately his poems consisted of short, erratic lines spread over the white page like scattershot. The words had started existing in isolation for him. The poetry, it seemed to him, was in the word itself, surrounded by white. Why tart it up? Critics (the few that bothered to consider the work of a vaguely noted academic poet) described his latest efforts as "laundry lists." When the cops had showed up at his door he'd been playing with that notion: Cling. Short Cycle. Press, Permanent.

He'd taken off his reading glasses and rose, with effort, to get the door. Everything lately was with effort. He seemed to sigh and grunt as part of his normal breath now. The accused assumed his ex-wife would be at the door, bringing him cookies left over from some volunteer function at the animal shelter. Theirs was a comfortable relationship of light mutual contempt that drummed on them bracingly like a light rain when they were together. The old demons of their relationship were soggy but still smelled alluringly like hellfire. As he walked toward the door he looked forward to seeing her, to possibly offending her, to maybe arguing a bit about their son (a psychology student who avoided seeing both of them, except on holidays).

Instead, it was two uniformed officers. They wanted to talk to him about a woman named Jillian. Would he come to the station? Jillian, he thought. How exotic of her to appear at the door, in this guise, in the mouths of these two strange men. He could hear his heartbeat for a moment, the blood rushing in his ears. The two men watched him and he nodded, keeping his lips tight over his teeth. Trouble was, he was getting a light, heady feeling, a bubble of euphoria that would break over his face in a weird short laugh or some out-of-line comment. He climbed into the cop car like a five-year-old being driven around in a cruiser as a wish fulfilled. Did he bounce a bit on the seat? Run his hands over the cage that separated him from the officers? He may have.

The scenes of his town—the gas station where he filled up, the coffee shop where he read the Sunday *Times*, the park where he jogged—all seemed transformed through the windows of the cruiser. He felt like a posthumous version of himself taking a tour of his old earthbound life. When they stopped at a red light by a corner bakery where he often ate a midmorning cinnamon roll, he looked in the window and could have sworn he saw himself, staidly working toward the center of the pastry (for he was like that—taking his pleasures in careful increments). He laughed as the cruiser thrummed forward and took him farther away from his daily circuit.

He sat in his recliner with a pile of poems and thought back to the station. It had been fascinating. The way they looped their questions around, asking him the same thing two or three times from different angles. How long have you known Jillian? When did you last see her? You last saw her on Friday? So after seeing her Friday, you did what again? Three days after that you got the Sunday *Times*? Where did you go Saturday? He liked the repetitive tattoo of the questions, how each one would pick up a theme from the last and give it a little twist. The two officers traded off so smoothly, and their voices and faces registering nothing the whole time. That flat affect combined with the inherent urgency in their long line of questioning struck him. "Hold back here," he wrote in the margin of one overheated student poem. "Try repeating this," he wrote on another. "Put this part behind a mask," he scribbled at the bottom of a long stanza. These were better comments than he usually gave.

What is your relationship with Jillian? That seemed to be the cops' favorite question, and he found it was one he liked considering. For what was his relationship with this troubled former student? They were both citizens of existence (that phrase being the name of his first slim volume of poems), their physical selves made circles around the same city park; they walked over each other's tracks, they were hit by the same sunlight, slightly altered by the curve of the earth. When he saw her that evening she was staring at a new sign in the park by the pond—No Dogs Allowed in Pond Area. She was wearing a beige shirt and pants and evening was falling, so from behind her figure curved in a hand-worn way, like a bone letter opener eroded at the middle from a frequent grip. For some reason, that evening, he decided he'd talk to her again. Everyone needs some shaking up. The poems blinking on his screen at home could use it. This mopey girl could use it. In fact, he thought, the night itself could use it. He used to love walking around alone in the park in the evenings, thinking of his poetry or his lovers (hadn't had one of those in a while), breathing in that sense of promise. Now the nights just seemed like a time when life went subterranean and damp, a plunge into black that left the next day dingier.

He walked up behind her just as she reeled her head back to spit. She was a good aim. The street light caught the saliva as it slid into the grooves of the sign. When she turned to him he could see, in the light, a froth of spittle on her lower lip. She smiled, widely, and wiped her mouth with the back of her hand. "Bullshit," she said, "All those dirty Canadian geese get the red-carpet welcome, but my dog can't walk ten feet from the thing? Ah yes, it's just *so* pristine."

He recognized in her voice the sound of someone off the rails, a sound he occasionally heard in other students over the years. There was so much variety, he thought, in how people veered off the path. The mumbling student of today who writes only about vegetation is the bipolar addict of tomorrow. The young man who always breaks in without raising a hand now collects bottles and plasters the town with political ads for a long-shot independent. The chubby girl with the immutable stanza length grows up to be a cloying and obsessive mother to a brilliant child-songstress who leaves the earth a thief and runaway. He had heard updates like these, along with updates of book deals and teaching gigs and happy scribblers and the like. He laughed at the goose comment warmly. He'd like to hear her keep going, watch her bounce off one irrational thought to the next. Prose-poem wild.

Had she ever visited his home? He drew a breath before answering, liking the effect. They walked through the dark park together, sort of. Jillian and the dog followed him as if it were happenstance. He looked behind him several times to confirm they were coming. "How is the journalism coming?" he called out in a rich, loud voice. Sometimes he enjoyed being loud around his more gossamer students; he liked to let his voice rip through them and leave their delicate sensibilities flapping in the breeze. She just laughed, and baby-talked to the dog. They left the park, wove through the neighborhoods with their little jockeys on the lawn and eagles above the garages. When he unlocked his door and turned around he expected her to be gone, but she and the dog bounded up the stairs and past him. He sat on an old wood rocker and she on the couch. He produced a drink and she sipped it and looked up.

The two cops leaned forward, almost imperceptibly. He could feel them becoming especially alert, as if someone were slowly turning a tuning peg on them and drawing them taut. This was a feeling he longed to produce in his readers, longed to produce in students, and longed to produce in himself. When had he really paid attention? He had when Jillian was there. He wanted to split through the muck of her hyper-private mental ills and have her listen to him.

This had been a bit of an obsession with him over the years. Once, visiting New York City on a self-funded book tour years ago, he engaged a street performer (a man spray painted in white posing to match a variety of statuary—Michelangelo's *David*, *The Thinker*, The Discus Thrower, even the Venus de Milo, which he recreated by clever contortions of the shoulder and elbow). He dropped a ten in the coffee can at the man's feet and then started talking to him. The man was happy to take a break and have a willing ear, and he told the accused all about the symbols inscribed inside every statue all over the world (yes, marble statues, despite the heft, are hollow), the scattered code that foretold of stock market secrets and the end of the world or some such thing. The man coughed a white cloud of dust and wiped his mouth, exposing a lushly pink inch of lip. Then he talked about the cops, how he performed only in their blind spot, the one part of the city where their surveillance fell short.

He had tried to engage the performer in some other kind of talk, something other than street-person raving. It wasn't that he wanted to talk sense into him—he didn't care—but he wanted to break through what seemed to him the man's disturbing sovereignty. The performer spoke as if he were reciting a poem pulled from memory. It was as if the accused wasn't even there. He argued with the performer at first, tried to anger him, then agreed with everything he said, attempting to shock him with sudden empathy. But nothing could faze him. Eventually the accused's now ex-wife grabbed him roughly by the shoulder and made him leave.

He envied crazy people, he realized, as he watched Jillian sip her drink. They really *bought* themselves. They bought their own logic, their own readings of the world, their own selves, regardless of how damaged they might seem to outsiders. "So," he began, unsure of what to say, "do you ever consider going back to poetry?" This wasn't the question he wanted to ask—he had no idea what to ask—and he hated his professorial tone. Jillian said nothing. She hummed to herself and wiggled her left hand at the dog. It was then he decided he would not say another word to her. Surely she expected him to speak, to do the work of the encounter. She probably thought he would talk poetry, or try to seduce her, or mentor her, or some wretched combo. All his actions, in her mind, were a foregone conclusion. He hated the thought of it. What could he do that would tip the picture?

Without a word he left her in the living room and walked into his office to think. The books of poems on the walls were no help. No stanza would be of use. There was an old-fashioned heavy iron used as a doorstop on the corner of his desk. Certainly, in the moment before one dies, her true face is shown. Who knows what insights might be glimpsed? That's probably what drove killers as much as the power or thrill or money or anything else. That ability to see into someone at the moment of supreme vulnerability. But he hadn't touched the iron—a goofy kitsch thing his ex-wife had gotten him. Janice liked to give him a gift on every anniversary of their divorce, usually something that had to do with a woman's woeful role in a marriage. She tied a bow on the iron and left it outside his office door at work, where he tripped over it while talking about the risks of frequent line breaks to a student with a long blond braid who had followed him so he could finish his thought.

But here in his home office, he could think of no next move. He kept scanning his shelves and noticed the Scrabble box, nearly obscured underneath a stack of files. He couldn't remember the last time he'd played—perhaps it was when he and Janice were still together and Henry still lived at home. Theirs was not a game-playing family, though, at least not in the wholesome sense, and he could hardly recall a time when the three of them sat facing one another. He grabbed the box and walked back to the living room. Jillian was still there, drinking and looking serene. In the indoor light he noticed a spray of moles across her cheekbones, like paint flicked off a brush.

"Back already?" she asked, and he simply nodded. The vow of silence felt good. He opened the box and laid out the Scrabble board at her feet. He divvied out her letters and his. Inexplicably she left the chair and dropped to the floor on her side of the board. The dog settled into the carpeting as if readying himself for a long night. When she touched the first letter—an I—their DNA mingled on her skin. And when he began telling the cops about the silent game of Scrabble, he could feel the exchange of glances between them, like a ripple of heat off summer pavement. So the two of you just played Scrabble and didn't speak? the boyish one asked, in a peevish and doubting tone. The sergeant tempered the question with a sotto voce request: Tell us about the game.

The accused shifted his feet. His shirt felt sweaty against the plastic chair, and the overhead lamp, while not as glaring as in the movies, still shed a stark bluish light that made his head hurt. Yet he didn't want to give up the chance to explain the game, its languid oddity, and its right-note-ness. He began the game with a weak word—something like *tea*—and Jillian crossed it with *taille*, an archaic tax, and he laid down *lathe* and she *egret*. He kept watching the words, feeling a pattern was about to emerge, some message or something. It felt like he was watching the pointer move around a Ouija board. At any moment he would be struck with some shocking reference. Jillian chuckled lightly to herself and ran her hands through the dog's fur over and over, so that her fingers disappeared and resurfaced like twin bottlenoses at the base of the dog's tail. Alright, Mr. Gelt, you're telling me you said nothing? I tell you what, you can't play a silent Scrabble game. What happens when you need to argue that something is really a word? You're telling me that didn't happen this game?

No, they just played. The tiles clicked. The words built. He kept score on a little pad of paper in her sight. He filled her drink once. He filled his twice. When the game was over (she won) she made a smooching noise at the dog, who sprang up as if he had long awaited the cue. She waved goodbye and walked out like nothing happened.

And then? "I went to bed," the accused said, his face suddenly hot, the room suddenly small.

When Jillian left, he had packed up the game and surprised Janice at her apartment. She was three sheets to the wind and cussing someone out on the phone when she answered the door. "And that's the end of that shit," she said, hanging up. "Scrabble! Honey, you didn't!" She always acted as if everything was a surprise when she was drunk. The two of them played a raucous game, shouting archaic words at each other until they both lost track of the points. At one point he grabbed her ponytail and made as if to kiss her. The closer he got the more he felt ill; getting close to her was as grotesquely intimate and satisfying as digging out an ingrown hair. She was a part of him, not in a romantic sense, but in the sense that being with her was a variation on being alone.

"I *heard.*" Janice called him when she found out. "How could they . . ." He heard her voice on the phone, sounding strange in its sincerity. Even when the marriage ended she was exhilarated in the courthouse, as if the divorce was a stage she had been pulled up onto by a crowd-pleasing magician. Her ceaseless levity wore him out, and his poems got heavier over the years simply to keep his mind from floating off into her particular toxic ether. So to hear her concern— the real fear—was a tonic. "Surely you told them about the Scrabble game? Where you were?" He assured her he told them about that night's Scrabble. The game was in a Ziploc somewhere. On some of those tiles the fingerprints overlapped like the same field tilled three times over, starting from different points.

He watched the dark streets outside his window, waiting for the return of the cruiser, the sluicing of slow tires in the damp street, the siren yip as the brakes engage and the car glows with the light of his file on the inboard screen. A man jogged by with a small dog struggling to keep up, its movement more side-to-side than forward, as if it were being twisted on a spit. He turned away, walked to the mirror in the hall. He put his wrists together in front of, then behind, his back.

Which was best? In front implied a willing giving over, an offering. Yet to hold his hands behind him was also a submissive gesture, he noted, since it took both his arms away from him. It would make him more streamlined, like a little blade or fin. He could choose to be pulled forward, or pushed. Either way he would enter the apparatus that would take him to his fate. He imagined it would be like riding in a car as a child, half asleep. He would be bumped and jarred, his head would be heavy, and he might hang from the seat belt in a stupor as the headlights raked over him in cascading geometries. And they would keep asking questions in their sonorous adult voices, about where he had been, what he had done, how things had gone. He always liked that.

IMPROVISATION

The play was a success, and all the actors crowded into the green room, gasping and talking loudly, still projecting as if on stage, their individual voices flung over each other like grappling hooks thrown to opposite ledges. The success was made all the sweeter by all the ways it was nearly not. Rosie, the lead, is grinning and crying with relief and exultation, and a long eyeliner drip changes course as she throws her head back to laugh: "The knocking was supposed to happen *after* Gracie tells me about what happened with the baby. But I start hearing this knocking *before* she even gets a line out! So get this," Rosie raises her voice—she is taking too long and losing listeners. "I start stomping on the floor! To cover up the sound of the knocks! And I explain it by saying I'm trying to confuse the termites. And Gracie says. . ."

The rest is lost as all attention moves to John, who is red-faced and sweating, squatting and gesturing at an invisible object that he marks out with two forefingers in the air. "I was supposed to pick up a *vase* on the sideboard and explain how fragile it is . . . You know, like a damn metaphor." He looks over his shoulder to be sure everyone is listening. "Well, I get going on my spiel and walk over to the sideboard and . . . no vase! No nothing! So I'm stuck explaining how fragile the damn *sideboard is*! And let me tell you, that thing doesn't look too fragile." He throws his hand at the mimed sideboard with a kind of playful faux-despair.

Two actors argue loudly enough to turn heads. In their scene, a wall of the set came down and they had to jump aside. Glen had continued with his lines as if nothing had happened. The other, Hal, had exclaimed about the "shoddy-ass slum-lord run pit," that is, he responded by responding in character. Glen has a glass of wine in his hands and shakes it to make a point. "Responding to the falling of the set at all takes the audience out of the moment. It acknowledges the artifice!" Hal is bent over the party tray, and sweat shakes off his mustache at every word. "Looks worse to ignore it." They continue to argue as everyone leaves the green room and walks the light-slicked streets to the after party, where there are more flushed faces and rousing stories of all the ways the play was saved, the mishaps taken in nonplussed stride, the wrong lighting cues, the lost props, the badly timed entries, the stage-frightened, the missed lines and too-soon departs. A thin young man, Jack, with a congratulatory rose snapped off in his buttonhole, laughs and tells his stories, listens to the others, and leaves finally for home with the sense of loss that always follows even a good show.

"But I must insist, Cecil . . ." As he walks he begins reciting lines from the play, of which he had precious few as the nephew of the patriarch who was written in late only to move the plot along; most of his lines were in the order of "But the Duke was just here!" or "I thought I saw the Mistress in the garden that very night!" and "*This* was left on the davenport!" He repeats all seven of them over and over, like a miser wrist-deep in a pile of coins, pulling up to hear them drop. The street is mostly dark, and the streetlights go out one by one; in fact they go out as he approaches. He keeps on. There is a place he often goes for drinks, but when he gets there it is no longer a decades-old neighborhood bar but an ice-cream parlor. He shrugs and gets a late-night cone. He walks and walks too far; the night wind whips the stem of his rose back and forth so fast it becomes a blurred arc, like a hummingbird treading air. He is lost. He looks around and sees his neighborhood rising above in the background as if it's a city in the sky resting on the rooftops of the neighborhood he's in. He can just see the molding around the top window of his apartment, the highest frond of his rubber plant. But there seems to be no way through; he darts back and forth across the street, his path like a stitch drawing the two curbs closed.

Suddenly he is flying through the air, not toward his apartment in the sky but away from it. He sees the stars between his toes. It is like the trick with the wires when Grace as the angel is sent to tell the Duke a message from his dead mother—a horribly trite moment, but the way the angel swings and pinwheels from her waist is almost worth it. Tonight her harness slid down to her upper leg, changing her pivot point, so that she somersaulted completely backward and had to deliver her lines at the Duke's feet through gossamer and netting while her naked legs pedaled above. Still she maintained her prophetic sweetness.

He makes contact and crumples like a time-lapsed closing rose. The stars he sees are now interwoven into one cyclopic light, the kind that keeps you from seeing the audience. The blood in his eyes becomes a smokescreen behind which the scene is switched. The curtain is hit from the inside and buckles out in momentary ripples; a thin shelf of light projects outward between the fringe and the floor, the big dark shapes lurch and scrape. He must respond. Continuity was the name of the game. If you ever paused too long on stage, if you were ever thrown . . . he thinks of the messenger, who stood at the door to the Duke's place, parcel in hand, and the slight obligation of saying, "A package for you, Duke," but who froze under the pressure nonetheless. His silence, the vicarious shame of the whole room, the poised moment that went on and on wobbling and circling its conclusion while no one took a breath . . .

His soul is working itself free of his body, like an actress snaking her way out of a tight, long dress with two stage hands pulling on the hem. With a great and violent undulation he is almost out, but in a heroic moment his body sits bolt upright and grabs the soul by the wisp of its trailing end, pulls it down, and cups it in his hand with a beatific, civic-minded smile, like this is the great opening of a public affair and he is in possession of the dove to be symbolically released. He lets go like he means to do it. In the empty orchestra pit, the void pads in and picks up the toothpicks and gum wrappers, music stands, and whatever else, then hangs there, like a custodian getting some shut-eye propped on two folding chairs. Even the celestial choir begins with coughs and laughs and people losing their place.

THE SLIDE TURNED ON END

We were sitting in his home office in Concord, Massachusetts. O'Hara —a biologist by trade—explained his entry into the art world. "I was on my way to a conference on DNA lithography in Illinois, when I got lost. I stopped at an art museum, called the conference directors, and realized that I got the day and time wrong. I missed the damn thing."

O'Hara gave a little shameless smile, acknowledging that brilliant minds are allowed leniency in planning and daily alertness. "So I figured, what the hell, I'll look around for a bit, I guess. And what I saw there was nothing short of remarkable." O'Hara, a rather shrunken man in his mid-sixties, spread his arms wide to show how wide-reaching his ideas were. "I saw science and art merge once and for all..."

O'Hara claimed he glanced at a work of abstract art—a Kandinsky, he thinks—and was immediately struck by how similar it was to some of the rare amoebas he was working with at the time. "I thought I was hallucinating. I mean, here was something precisely like what I had under the slide just that morning!" So precise was the resemblance that he thought he had lost his mind. "I nudged this person next to me and said—I mean, I realize how absurd this is now—I said, 'Is that a blown-up slide of Grayson's amoeba, I mean, is that the guy's er ... inspiration?'" O'Hara reported that all he got in response was an "I think not" and some advice about brushing up on his art history. O'Hara, however, was sure that he had hit upon something significant. "The more I walked around looking at this so-called abstract art, the more I felt like I was looking at a bunch of blown-up slides turned on end." When he returned to his university, he quickly arranged a sabbatical to study this phenomenon. "I lied to the department. I said I was going to study a new way to extract antibodies from fungi—specifically, truffles. There's no way I would get a sabbatical to look at a bunch of art." He was clearly pleased at his effortless deception. "Those morons heading up that department haven't a clue. I used all the truffles they ordered for me to make dinner for a group of art critics."

Clearly, these truffle dinner parties were a success, because soon O'Hara had created a buzz among art critics. By this point, he had firmed up his idea. "I realized we humans probably react to art because we must, in some subconscious way, recognize it. Even abstract art. What I'm saying is I think we can sense the tiniest part of ourselves, and our origins—the cells, platelets, and our amoeba ancestors—in these images. And I think that's what resonates with us when we view abstract art. We are, in a sense, recognizing the bits." At first blush, this hardly seemed like the type of theory to garner any sort of following. The fact that it did might be more a reflection of the art world's permanent scramble for the "new" than a reflection of its merits. Still, O'Hara was prepared for resistance. "Look, I know this theory is hard to accept. We all want to believe that we appreciate art because it's 'beautiful' or somehow or other special and apart from our daily lives. But the fact is we appreciate it because it's life—only magnified."

I must have dropped my neutral reportage face because before I knew it, O'Hara was leading me down to his basement, where he housed his "evidence." "Look at this." He produced a glossy photo of a striated blob. "This is a virus—the common flu, to be exact. And now look at *this*." He now pulled out a reproduction of Paul Klee's work. "Is that uncanny or what?" There was a slight resemblance of line quality, but uncanny seemed like an overstatement. Always alert to skepticism, O'Hara supplied the explanation. "If that virus was just a hair turned right, and caught during a moment of replication, it would match the Klee painting exactly." He then produced a Helen Frankenthaler and sighed with relish at how much it reminded him of hemoglobin. "It reminds me of some of my first real moments at the 'scope," O'Hara reminisced, using a shortened form of "microscope" to indicate both his familiarity with and affection for the device. "We were supposed to find irregularities in rat blood supplies. I remember thinking how beautiful these irregularities looked, even though I knew they indicated hemophilia, and thus the end of the rat." At this, he gave me a significant look as if he knew he inadvertently linked death and beauty but wanted to leave the implications of *that* for later. He instead bent down and rifled through more drawers, producing slides, prints, and photos that he laid out in a meticulous display of resemblances. O'Hara went on to compare this who's who of abstract art to what he assured me was a who's who of bacteria, protozoa, and cells. Here and there the resemblances truly were uncanny, but what that proved remained obscure.

Microaestheticism may seem, at times, big on evidence but short on implications—of course, comparing abstract art to microorganisms might show similarities, but what does that ultimately mean? Other art critics have criticized O'Hara for creating a theory that cannot be properly applied—once you believe that abstraction is a yearning for our minute origins, what more is there to do or say? O'Hara, still a man of science, bristled overtly at that claim. "Look, I'm a biologist. Everything I do must have an outcome and a methodology. Microaestheticism is no exception. It is, in fact, far more rigorous than anything that passes for a theory in the art world now." O'Hara quickly brightened at his insult of art theory and suggested we go to his lab to see the "practice" of Microaestheticism.

Markus O'Hara's "lab" is not really a lab at all—after being ousted from his university for the fruitless (at least in traditional biology terms) and fraudulent sabbatical, O'Hara took up with a sympathetic group of critics who used their university ties to secure a space for

O'Hara's research. "No one in the sciences wanted anything to do with me. I was a defector." Typical of O'Hara, he described all of his rejections as reflections of the small-mindedness and fear of those who turn him away. "They were nervous. I was applying science to the indeterminacy and chaos of art. I was collapsing the walls between them." He dropped his voice conspiratorially as he explained the deeper reason for their fear. "And you know what? Sometimes I think science is nothing more than maintaining those walls—asserting that it's *not* art, *not* religion, *not* philosophy. All their work is to prove their separateness. And I want to show science's connectedness—the places where everything overlaps."

O'Hara's allies in art could only provide support from their world, so his lab was a studio before he crudely converted it for his purposes. Extension cords ran willy-nilly over the floor, some connecting to a power source or a device and others purely aesthetic, serving nothing but the compositional effect of another curving line. Thin wires and small pipes also ran the length of the room, giving the whole place the look of a magnified network of nerves set aquiver by the latest stimuli. The hub of the lab was centered on a few battered stainless steel tables topped with a lineup of microscopes of differing repair and size. The walls of the space were covered with reproductions of art and tiny pictures of various magnifications of some "bit" with nothing but the captions 200×, 300×, 400× as identification. O'Hara ushered me over to a microscope.

"It's not a fully equipped lab, to be sure. But I have most of what I need. It can be dangerous here, though. To tell you the truth, this space isn't at all set up for something to go wrong."

I noticed an emergency shower station in the far corner, but before I could point out that he at least had that for safety's sake, O'Hara laughed. "That's not a real shower station. That's a sculptural piece meant to show how empty our ideas of security are. In fact, if you turn it on, it releases a noxious cloud of pepper spray." O'Hara seemed unfazed by the possibility of being left with nothing but a safety parody in a lab crisis. "I think it's a stunning piece. It's by Mave Aieka. Heard of her?"

Of course I had heard of her—she was simply the latest in a long line of trend-riding assemblageists. But O'Hara's name-dropping indicated that he was becoming a full-fledged member of the art world, even as his ties to science become more tenuous. Perhaps sensing that he was treading too far into the art side of things, O'Hara made a show of his expertise at the 'scope. He fiddled with various knobs, putting his face to the eyepiece periodically to check on the adjustment. Sometimes he winced at what I assumed was a blurry image, and other times he smiled slightly, as if a particularly sought-after blob had just reached the proper crispness. Eventually, he said "look" in a hushed tone and gestured toward me, as if the microscope contained something wild and beautiful and capable of being startled away. And what I saw was indeed beautiful. Three organic shapes in sage, azure, and copper undulated into a picture of ever-increasing compositional sophistication. A stringy offshoot produced a pleasing diagonal line, while the greenish blob shifted into a deepening plane. It truly looked like a highly accomplished work of abstract expressionism. But then the forms shifted again, and the image now resembled the mawkish fumbling of a first-year art student, resorting to abstraction not out of passion but out of an inability to master the basics of realism.

O'Hara, with an uncanny ability to preempt my comments, summed up the experience. "I know. It's beautiful for a moment and then it's garbage. That's the problem with organic, living matter. But you want to know what those were under there?" He waited for me to supply the superfluous "what?" while I waited for him to give up and continue without it. We broke down simultaneously, both of us suddenly speaking at once. For a moment O'Hara seemed annoyed, but the thought of his theory, as always, seemed to banish all irritation from his mind. "Those were my own cells you were looking at. My own cells, that is, after visiting the museum." O'Hara delivered this with a finality that indicated that I should find this as significant as he did. With a slight hand-flutter of impatience, O'Hara elucidated. "You see, I went to the museum, and I swear to the holy higher power that my cells, blood, skin, tissue, the whole bit—became *like art after viewing the art*. What I'm saying is—and I know this sounds radical—I'm proposing that our organic selves adjust to art. We see the art, and our bits then become the art. Our body *recognizes* abstraction and, in turn, competes with it."

O'Hara now seemed to be entering some even stranger theoretical territory than before. Was he just synthesizing a number of clichés and new-agey superstitions into one pithy idea? We're beautiful on the inside, art is good for the soul, and we're all unique—all repackaged as Microaestheticism. Was this a ploy to sell the theory, to give it some marketable touchy-feelyness?

O'Hara, however, seemed too sincere and unsavvy for such salesmanship. He was still lost in explaining the before and after appearance of his cells. "They were downright boring before. I mean, they were drab. My skin cells were just beige little irregular chambers, my blood cells were completely uninspired. Even the bacteria in my gut looked hackneyed. They were nothing, nada, sans thing, el nothito." O'Hara apparently found some amusement in approximating other languages, an unusual quirk for someone of his education. "But afterwards . . ." He paused to give his customary lovelorn sigh. "They were sublime."

"Hey—I've got an idea." At once overtaken by manic energy, O'Hara began rummaging through the boxes piled about the studio. As his search intensified, he became less concerned with keeping things orderly. He knocked images off the wall as he rushed by without even bothering to see what he had unsettled. At one point, he toppled a rickety microscope but merely giggled when it hit the floor. "Mave can have that one," he said, referring to his sculptress friend. "She's been planning on creating a 'scope sculpture as a criticism of the fussy, mechanical way gallery-goers see art. She'd love the big lenses on that one." Finally, in the bottom of what looked like a tackle box, O'Hara's search ended. "We've got to get a blood smear from you," O'Hara blurted, simultaneously casting me as both a fellow researcher and willing test subject. "It's perfectly safe." O'Hara punctuated this by showing me a trio of lancets, still in their sterile wrapping. "I would love, love, love to get a look at your blood. I'm sure it's spectacular. After all the art you've seen . . ." He virtually shuddered with pleasure at the thought. Both flattered and curious, I held out my arm for him.

"Wait." He again launched into a search, this time for something he called Ethiphet©. "Where is the goddamn Ethiphy?!" This search, much shorter than the last, quickly produced a vial of absinthe-hued liquid from the recesses of a clearly secondhand file cabinet. "Now just drink this first. It's a stabilizing agent. Sort of like a coagulant but not quite. What it does is slow the movement of your blood cells so they'll fix into an image under the slide." Unconsciously, I had drawn my arms back to my body protectively, the arm formerly offered up now receding behind my back. Another impatient flutter of hands. "For god's sake, of course it's safe. It's sure as hell safer than all the genetically modified food you scarf down without a thought! I'm a biologist. I know the properties of everything in this lab down to the molecule! And I know their effects!" O'Hara's presumptuousness about my eating habits (scarf?) made me even less inclined to take the "Ethiphy." "Look. You saw what happened under that slide. The cells shift, the picture's ruined. Don't you want to see how beautiful your cells could really look? Who knows? You might be a masterpiece." O'Hara whispered this last part in my ear, after silently advancing into my space.

The old observation about people eventually coming to resemble their pets seems doubly true for theorists and their theories. Wittgenstein was as austere and difficult as his theories, living in a highly ordered home and quick to anger over unintelligible slights. Kierkegaard's theories were innately paradoxical, much like his sex life: he would woo, woo, woo, and then cut out before consummation. (Some biographers claim to have found evidence that Kierkegaard had a curved penis, which would explain his sexual reticence. Even that deformity could be seen as a metaphor for his ideas.) O'Hara himself, likewise, now seemed just as threatening to me as he claims Microaestheticism is to science. One could speculate that O'Hara wanted a unified front: man and theory, both at the ready to disturb. And finally illuminate.

Ultimately, though, neither O'Hara nor Microaestheticism presented any real danger. Or any real illumination. Microaestheticism may be a pleasant diversion, but it simply stands on too many thresholds to truly enter into theoretical discourse. Part science, part art criticism, part New Age feel-goodism, part old-time alchemy. But in the all: not much. The mainstream art world simply won't accept that its field is mere inaccurate biology, and if O'Hara's old colleagues are any indication, science will simply banish it, not even granting the acknowledgment of a refutation. It seemed harmless enough, then, to follow O'Hara's instructions, if only to fully experience what will no doubt come to be known as an amusing hiccup in the history of ideas.

The Ethiphet© went down easily and seemed to have a numbing effect. O'Hara had already deftly pricked the finger by the time I put the vial down. "It works the minute it hits the gullet," he said, without explaining this improbability or apologizing for what felt like a pretty rude way to take a blood sample. Wasn't there a blood-taking etiquette? Unlike someone in the medical profession, who would at least put on an empty show of caring about my well-being (or give some vague comforting comment such as "that wasn't so bad, was it?"), O'Hara had already moved on, with nary a half-hearted nicety. For lack of a cotton ball or a Band-Aid, O'Hara absently reached over, without taking his eyes off the lancet, and ripped off a paper towel from a soiled-looking roll. But perhaps O'Hara could be excused (or figured he should be) for all his born-of-distraction boorishness: he was, of course, a man of both science *and* art, leaving little for the prosaic world of manners, bedside or otherwise.

O'Hara now silently drew the lancet, sheathed thinly with a spread drop of blood, along a slide, then pressed another slide atop it to secure the sample. He slipped the specimen into its proper place under the 'scope lens, securing it with two silver clips. With the herky-jerkyness of someone tired of simply verging on something great, O'Hara nearly leaped to the other side of the table and thrust his head at the eyepiece. He hit it with what looked like enough force to give himself a black eye, yet he didn't pull back to assess the damage or rub his eyes in chagrined bafflement. Instead, he merely grunted with impatience and reached down to reaffix the slide. Now came another round of ever-so-slight knob spinning, focusing, and refocusing. To the untrained observer he appeared to be undoing everything he did, as every knob turn seemed followed by a knob turn of an equal amount in the opposite direction. To O'Hara, though, progress was being made. Soon enough, he chortled and pulled his hands away from either side of the 'scope to free them up for a merry clap of victory. "Come here," he called, his voice taking on the near-obscene vibrato of intense pleasure. "It's as beautiful as I had hoped."

But the trek to the microscope, and the image, seemed suddenly complicated. For one thing, there were suddenly two of everything: two Dr. O'Haras, two battered stainless steel tables, two identical 'scopes. Though disorienting, it certainly had its implications for O'Hara's work. He probably *would* benefit from having two selves— one to remain in the science world and one to flee fully into art.

The whole room now shifted entirely out of focus, as if the whole space was under a giant 'scope, and O'Hara, miscalculating, turned a mammoth knob way too far. It took considerable effort to keep O'Hara in my vision—there was suddenly something indistinct about him. Much like Microaestheticism, which more and more seemed to me a theory only of specifics, lacking a fundamental to give those fine points relevance, O'Hara's relationship to the space was suddenly unclear. Was he that form inches to my right? Or was he the faded blob still feet away? Groping, like all theories do in their infancy, I reached out for my bearings and apparently collided with the 'scope instead.

"Damnit! I had it perfectly adjusted! Look, this space is just as sacred as any gallery. Same rules apply! Watch what you're doing; don't touch without permission," O'Hara scolded. "This place may not be pretty but there's serious stuff going on here. You can't just grab at things willy-nilly." O'Hara seemed unduly annoyed, as if he had been intuiting my increasing doubts about his theory and his credibility. Perhaps that's why he elaborated so unnecessarily. "Think about it. What if you just reached out like that in a gallery and knocked over a sculpture?" Leaving me to think about what I had done, O'Hara went back to his adjustment ritual. The knobs turned, a sound not unlike an arthritic joint complaining at having to move once more. Or perhaps that sound *was* O'Hara's joints, the soft bone-on-bone groan of a body too often employed in the same tiny gestures. In the absence of any clear visuals, it was impossible to say which. But it was clear where the murmurs of complaint originated. O'Hara's mutters, theatrically overblown to remind me of the grievous consequences of my conduct, ranged from snarled "damnits" to little whispers on how things had degenerated in the last minute. "Well, there goes the right quadrant," he said, seeming to address the 'scope in their kindred agony over how out of whack everything had become. But as for O'Hara's face and movements, they were left up to guesswork. The room remained as undefined as the moment of my transgression.

"All right. It's as fixed as it's going to be. Believe me, it's not nearly as good as it was *before*, but it'll at least give you some indication of the quality of post-art-viewing blood." I advanced toward the sound of O'Hara's voice gingerly—I had a feeling bumping the 'scope a second time would be more than enough ground to end our contact. As I attempted to round the corner of the steel table to the viewing side, I felt O'Hara's hand close around my upper arm. "Open your eyes, will you? You were about to bump the table." O'Hara, one of the few of us blessed enough to believe that everything he does is eye opening, luxuriated in the dual meaning of his directive. "You know, Microaestheticism is all about opening your eyes. It's about seeing life—and art—in a new and entirely synergistic way."

I stood in front of the 'scope, unable to decipher where it began or ended, or how far it was from my face. O'Hara, suddenly enthralled at what must be a new thought about his cherished theory, went on, oblivious to my hesitance. "In fact, I see the 'scope itself as a conduit to that new seeing. Unlike the gallery—with its white walls, its wine and cheese corner, its emptiness amplifying every insipid utterance— the 'scope is a quiet and private place." He paused to let the profundity of that sink in. "And I like that you have to bend down and put your eye to an eyepiece to see a slide. That act . . . it's like a literal— or rather—a literal*ized* gesture—or act—of interpretation." O'Hara, demonstrating the smug habit of rewording his own ideas merely to extend their expression, seemed in no hurry for me to begin this "act." And all this talk about seeing was providing too obvious an irony in a room now so blurry.

"You know, when you put your eye to the eyepiece, you actually bring your brain closer to the slide, you know, the art. Isn't that neat? That's really what you're doing at the 'scope—getting that thinker right up tight to the art." Merely to stop O'Hara from continuing down this line of thinking—a line that would no doubt lead to another manic epiphany about the implications of his Big Idea—I asserted my interest in finally seeing what all the fuss was about. "Well, by golly then, put your eye to the 'scope. You don't need my invitation. That's the thing about the 'scope. It, by its very mechanism, *demands* viewer participation. You have to crane down and look. You can't just stroll through like you can in a gallery. Noooope . . ." I had a feeling this was meant as some sort of dig—as if O'Hara was implying I had been spoiled by the noncommittal ease of gallery going. Rather than argue with him—perhaps pointing out that a viewer's level of engagement had nothing to do with a physical "craning" or lack thereof—I attempted to line up my eye socket with the eyepiece. It was best to let it go. O'Hara was obligated to criticize the art world; otherwise, how could he justify his intrusion? Like many theorists, O'Hara's zeal was born of a belief that his idea was a long-overdue corrective. And anyone who was presumptuous enough to believe himself capable of remedying both art and science would hardly be distracted by the pinpricks of a single doubter's logic.

A man of science, such as O'Hara still would tout himself, could probably tell me that looking through the 'scope's magnified lenses would not correct what had suddenly gone wrong with my vision. Still, once I finally situated my face on the eyepiece, I was startled to see nothing crisper than the general blur everything had become. I tried to tell O'Hara, but I suddenly was too short of breath to speak. Thankful for what he no doubt thought was a silence inviting commentary, O'Hara plowed forward with a fresh thought on his theory.

"You know what would really be great? To have a slide with a viewer's blood blown up right next to the picture he just saw. So, you have someone look at a Clyfford Still—let's say that big black one. 'Untitled' something or other. Then, you look at his blood under the slide, take a magnified picture of it, blow it up, and tack it up right there next to the Still painting. I bet the blown-up blood would look like the Still painting, only more advanced. Like the next aesthetic step." Gasping now, and doubled over in a barely repressed dry heave, I was forced merely to think my protests to this. O'Hara had a different reading of my response.

"Whoa there!" O'Hara reached out, grabbed my arm, and turned me around to face him. "Hey now, calm down. I know it's shocking to see that level of composition under a slide. Believe me, when I first placed a photo of blown-up intestinal flora next to a Gorky, I had about the same reaction. 'Bout had to breathe into a paper bag, to be frank." It always baffled me when people announced frankness about matters that demanded neither openness nor caginess. Whether or not he needed a paper bag after epiphany #453—and whether or not he was up-front about that fact or kept it tucked away in euphemism—seemed wildly beside the point as I was overtaken by a new round of heaves. Perhaps, I thought, feeling another contraction of my gut in protest to something likely more potent than any insight I heard today—perhaps O'Hara's thoughtless recasting of my physical trouble as awe at his idea indicated a larger paradox of great and small minds alike.

There seem to me two types of artists and thinkers. There are those who work under a heavy mantle of self-skepticism, barely able to plow through their own doubt enough to clear any room for their creations. Then, there are those who seem not to acknowledge—or perhaps even sense—any doubts whatsoever. This style of mind sees everything in the world as support for its creations. Even contradictory evidence, detractors, a whole world shouting "this is not so" seem only further proof that the world needs them. Otherwise, why wouldn't it already believe? Clearly, O'Hara was in the latter category: so romanced by his own thinking that even a totally unconnected phenomenon—such as a retching journalist—registered as a rising cheer for his theory. The problem is that it is hard to know which type of thinker to admire. At first, a skeptic's wise tempering of his or her own insights seems nobler, as he or she is at least acknowledging all human fallibility. But then the realization hits: both the skeptic and the believer are equally solipsistic, as the extreme nature of both their doubts and convictions can be born of nothing less than a mind untethered by outside reality.

Maybe this was why, even after sitting me down in a swiveling chair and rushing off to hunt down a paper bag, O'Hara hardly broke stride in his pontificating. "I have in my mind's eye a new art," O'Hara shouted from across the room, over the sounds of his own rifling. "Pigments in Petri dishes. Cells on canvas. Diseases exposed to art. Artists exposed to disease." O'Hara had now returned, and he shook out a paper bag inches from my bowed head (bowed, that is, not in reverence of Microaestheticism, but to ward off a wave of nausea and dizziness). "There might be a bit of powder left in this bag, but don't worry about it." O'Hara then jammed the bag on my face, kindly leaving it up to me to decide whether to christen it as a hyperventilation bag or a vomit bag. Not wanting to inhale, ingest, or otherwise encounter any more substances of O'Hara's, I brought up my arms and pushed it away, bringing on a new round of wheezing. "Suit yourself," O'Hara huffed. "It was just filled with harmless spores."

Insensitive is surely too mild a term for someone who begins discussing the beauty of disease in the face of true physical agony. But it was the only term I had the energy to supply as O'Hara elucidated his meaning. "See, you expose disease to art, and then check it under a 'scope. Is it more beautiful? Is it trying to outdo the art with its own composition of viruses, bacteria, or malignant cell overgrowth? I bet it is. Conversely, you could also look at the cells of ailing artists. How does the image of their disease size up to the average sufferers? The thing is . . ." Here, O'Hara lowered his tone, taking the manic lilt from his voice to show how admirably even-handed his consideration of these matters was. "I think we really need to answer these questions before we even *consider* treating disease with art or contracting disease for art's sake." *How prudent of you!* I badly wanted to quip, but it was a distant third on my list of present wants, after "to breathe" and "to see."

"Caught your breath yet?" O'Hara asked, in the offhand, rhetorical manner of someone asking if I was enjoying the weather of a perfect day. I opened my mouth to answer in the strenuous negative, but all that resulted was a series of hacking coughs followed by another ominous retch, this one ill-content to remain dry. As matter gurgled and rose up into my mouth, I covered my lips and forced it back down, where it rumbled, prophesizing another uprising. "You, my friend, need to be out of the vicinity of the 'scope when you erupt." O'Hara seemed to pack another aimless insult in his use of the crude, unsympathetic "erupt" to describe a body's natural revolt. He grabbed the back of my chair and rolled me to a corner, as if moving a piece of unneeded equipment out of the way. "I was not planning on this when I invited you here, you know. I'm not here to play school nurse."

Was it that reference to childhood, or something else, that suddenly prompted a montage of my growing up? Though seemingly still conscious, and still focused on the floor with my head bowed, and still slightly swiveling the swivel chair with every fought-down heave, I could suddenly see isolated images of my youth. I saw myself, four or five, finger-painting in a way not intended—delicately, using small parts of each finger for different colors, my fingernail employed as a crude spade to give the picture texture, and me, pausing for minutes at a time in contemplation of my next mark. I saw my art teacher, oblivious, leading me over to a classmate to show me how it's really done . . . and this kid, without the slightest plan in his mind, rubbing his entire hand and forearm in each color and slopping the muddy mix on paper, sometimes ripping it, sometimes missing it, and all the while grinning in that it's-damn-good-isn't-it way. So much like O'Hara was that baseless confidence, that idiotic pride in his every expression.

Then I saw myself, about twelve, at the scholastic art fair, jotting down flaws in the works I saw in a little field book. Little Holly Rander's "Two Faces"? *Too baroque! No one's eyelashes curl to that degree!* And Johnny Wiles's "My Mom, Dad, and Brother"? I remember my pleasure at coming up with: *All the sap of Norman Rockwell with none of the skill!* Then everything sped up, and it became harder to tell what time period images came from. Some were mere snippets—an exhibition catalogue falling to the floor, a fountain pen presented in a velvet case for a bygone birthday, an artist using the same circular gesticulation over and over to describe his series of tondo paintings, as if I needed his help to visualize "round." The visions kept coming, and nothing tied them with the present moment except that they were a showcase of a life absent of Microaestheticism, a life where a clear line was drawn between art and science, cells and paint, illness and art-making.

If Markus O'Hara had his way, no life-review hallucinatory episode would ever be without the firm presence of Microaestheticism. A memory of kindergarten would draw up a different method of finger-painting, one which owed a heavy debt to O'Hara and his theory. Kindergarteners would simply rub their bare hands—still with abandon, of course—over a line-up of slides, which they would then look at under a microscope to see what sort of image their skin cells, oil, and perhaps PB&J residue would create. "A more accurately dubbed 'finger painting,'" O'Hara would likely say of it. And a scholastic art fair? Maybe, rather than questioning the unearned sentiment of a colored-pencil family portrait, a young critic would comment on a diptych of a cartoon daisy and a few chambers of skin cells arranged to mimic it, pointing out that the resemblance between the two was too obvious to be evocative.

Perhaps that was, after all, the most damning criticism of Microaestheticism. Both the body, with its still-inchoate vagaries (ever mocking science), and art, in its untraceable power and inscrutable victories, still largely elude us, and rightfully so. To pin both art and science under a single slide, never allowing them free play in the unknown, is to sacrifice mystery for control. Still, when the vagaries of the body are upon us, when chests contract, when arms go numb, when vision falters, when retching asks for more than mere vomit, seeming to demand that the innards rise up in the throat as well—the mystery, admittedly, can be a bit hard to appreciate. But a critical mystery, I maintain, it nevertheless is. Through the in-and-out flickering that had now become my visual and aural field, I heard O'Hara, and as usual he hardly seemed to second me.

"Mmmm...," O'Hara began. "I think I know *exactly* what's going on here. You've been skeptical about Microaestheticism this whole time, and now you've seen proof—in the image of your own blood nonetheless—of its validity. So you play up a coughing fit to stall until you can think of some clever way to refute it. Not a gracious loser, eh?"

Playing up a coughing fit? Of course. No drama exterior to the drama in O'Hara's own mind could be anything but a ploy. "But I'm used to this stuff. Comes with the territory, as they say. But you *are* gonna look at the slide again. It's shifted into an even better composition. There'll be no denying it then, friend. No denying it then." His words were followed by a series of what felt like seismic shits, as my movement seemed to occur absent of my volition. "Oopsies," O'Hara said, as I felt my body hurl forward. "Gotta watch out for these cords. Up you go!" It occurred to me that O'Hara was likely pushing my chair, but when I tried to feel around me, no definitive conclusion could be made on that. "Final stop, 'Scope Terminal. Everybody off." I felt O'Hara grab me under my armpits and hoist me somewhere, presumably at the 'scope. I opened my mouth again in an attempt to impress upon O'Hara the gravity of my condition, but all that happened was a bubbling up of something bile-like, which I had barely the energy to choke down.

"*Look.*" I felt O'Hara's hands at the back of my neck and head, directing me into the proper craning at the 'scope. While he pushed down on the back of my head, presumably to line me up better with the eyepiece, the sudden force caused my legs to slide under me. As I felt myself oozing to the floor, like so much precious substance spilled from a beaker, O'Hara tightened his grip on my head. "Ah-ah-ah . . . you're not getting out of this so easily." At that, he pulled me up, cranium first, and again thrust me at the 'scope. "*Look.*" O'Hara moved in closer to support me, effectively jamming me between him and the table, while the 'scope served as a balance point for my head. I probably looked much like Dali's seeping clocks, kept only from puddling by their precise arrangement on the crutches. Such an image could double as a representation of theories, like Microaestheticism, that try to balance something as fluid as the sublime on something as rigid as fact.

As O'Hara pushed my head more firmly on the 'scope, my vision finally graduated from intermittent to all black. I was embarrassed to admit that my instinctive interpretation was utterly layman. "I have gone blind," I thought, falling prey to that stock reading of everything going dark. Not wanting to give O'Hara the satisfaction of pointing out a conventional interpretation (even in my inner monologue), I concentrated until the darkness become something more. Balanced on the scope, I suddenly saw something—a vague form, a patch of lighter dark—emerge from the otherwise consistent field. The image was similar to Ad Reinhardt's "Black Painting #34," with a ghost-of-a-form manifesting after enough concentration. It was a brilliant use of subtlety; a subtlety employed so successfully that it became more extreme than a white swath on a black canvas. The thing about blackness is that no one looks at it long enough; viewers assume there's nothing to see. But forming an image, even the shyest silhouette, in the language of black is more powerful than introducing color because it introduces the idea that there is no absolute saturation. Everything is a study in value.

If only I could have spoken then, I could have reached a tenuous common ground with O'Hara, conceding that what I saw under the slide was indeed spectacular, perhaps calling for a reevaluation of the worth of Microaestheticism, and thus forging a truce in awe. I tried to speak, but all I think I managed was "Blackkkkkkkkk . . . ," followed by a hot, wet clot spat up against the back of my teeth, which soon occupied all my energy in its gagging-down. O'Hara, still behind me to ensure I was wedged at the scope until I hit an acceptable epiphany about his work, saw this as a good time to make a pun. "Black? Hardly. For an art critic, you certainly have a limited 'palate' of words! Ha! To *me*, the real beauty of those cells is their almost utter transparency . . . Hmmmm . . . It's sort of like jellyfish layered upon jellyfish, upon jellyfish . . ."

"Upon jellyfish"—which sounded like a fit title for a Damien Hirst work—seemed to ricochet around the room, multiplying and becoming a sort of nonsense mantra, terrifying in both its implications and ultimate meaninglessness. Again, I felt myself sliding into an even worse conventional reading, both philistine and alarmist. *I'm blind!*

I'm dying! But I gamely pulled myself back: perhaps O'Hara, in a jittery haste, had just left the lens cap on. Perhaps that was the black I was seeing. I swung my head away from the 'scope to test this theory, before O'Hara grabbed my head and pushed me back. "C'mon now. What do you gotta say about this image now? Huh?" In that instant away from the scope, the blackness remained.

Yet it seemed too variously shaded to be blindness, too permeable to be the lens cap, too solid to be the image of my blood cells. It was something else, something that encompassed all those things but committed to none of them fully, or perhaps better said, committed to none of them *restrictively.* It was a rich overlay on the present moment, a cryptic light-blocking, oppressive, yet aesthetically one-upping every specific—blindness, the lens cap, blood cells—I could dream up as its source. It was, in essence, what art should be, what theory could be—an expanse outside all specifics. O'Hara, likely sensing how beyond him and Microaestheticism I now was, threw his hands up and let me finally fall. In that sweet drift away from the confines of theory to the release of art, I went over and over the options for what the darkness could be, granting, finally, that what it was *truly* was not as relevant as what it was *critically.* The blackness had achieved the only triumph to be had in art: an irreproachable ambiguity.

I tried to lift my arm to indicate that I was, in my own highly qualified way, a believer. Perhaps not in Microaestheticism and certainly not in O'Hara, but I did believe in the desire to extend the reach of art—to science, to the body, and beyond. But as I raised my arm in what was meant to be a sort of reverence for the communal enterprise of art-furtherance, my body chose to express this reverence in a far more explosive way. Blood shot from mouth like paint from a stepped-upon tube, my breath drew violently into my lungs, where it sulked, refusing to release itself in an exhale. Worst of all, the glorious blackness before me, with its eloquent language of value, was suddenly shot through by a blinding white light, the kind of impul-

THE SLIDE TURNED ON END

sive, stupid mark that instantly demotes a painting from masterwork to let's-get-out-the-gesso-and-start-again. The whiteness expanded, beckoned; like all bad art it was notable only in how blatantly solicitous it was of the viewer. Unlike bad art, however, this swath of white seemed to have the manpower to back it up, and drew me in and away despite myself.

"You mind if I use this stuff as a sample? It'll save me a lancet."

ORNAMENT AND CRIME

My father has died, and in my hand are his remains—ashes pressed and fired into a small flattish cube—and I'm laboring to insert him into something so that he sits flush. He always wished to be a geometric form (so often did he rail against "the tyranny of the organic" that I could tell myself he'd be happy), but he also hated bric-a-brac and I think right now he'd qualify, being a small object with no function. Better to join him with a nice flat plane. Shim up a gap on a sleek modernist home. There are plenty around here. Some are monolithic and shimmering, with metal roofs that sweep across the facades, the entrances coyly obscured. Others are crouched tightly to their lawns, their recessed windows narrowed and aglow.

I walk through the backyards, pretending to be a meter reader. I'm wearing Dad's red jumpsuit, the one he wore in prison, and a tool belt to complete the look. I stop and study each house. I pull out the cube and run it along siding, storm windows, blocks, etc., hoping to feel it dip into place. It does, in the back deck of a glass monolith, a house that resembles a drive-in movie screen upon which a scene of a Weimaraner darting between two midcentury daybeds repetitively plays. I almost leave him, but the cube looks too obvious in the space between boards.

Before he set our neighbors' dollhouse shed on fire using a plain silver Zippo (triumph of utilitarian design) and naphtha, we lived together in a Danish modern home. What I recall most was cleaning the stainless steel refrigerator, chasing a smudge of grease round and round, driving it across the surface with a Windexed rag only to have it reappear on the other side, so teasing and full of character it seemed like a friend. Then Dad went to jail. For him, prison was a revelation—he thrilled at the cells, with their efficient layouts, the clean-lined cinderblock walls, the low toilets, the austere bunks. The *iconic* red Princess phones, heavy with engineering, the Plexiglas, turned nicely matte from all the scratches. The *pleasingly unadorned* speech of prisoners.

The afternoon light quivers on the horizon edge of an infinity pool. Blocky red chaises sit in this backyard near cast-concrete stools made to look like tree stumps. I consider dropping him in the pool—it is a nice pool—and saying my goodbye into a swirl of deep-end bubbles. A safe place for the dead arsonist. I am holding him up to the sun, ready to let go, when a shadow crowds my peripheral. It's a man, dressed in a beige polo, rounding the corner. I step behind a streaky potted grass. The man is carrying a rake. With superfluous flourish, like someone signing an important document with a triumphant lift of the pen, he makes a small pile of silver leaves. Paid by the hour, my dad would say, not by the job.

I remember Dad running his hands over surfaces—our granite countertop had pink striations, like veins. When it was clean—which was often—he would run his palm, quickly, over the whole length and off the edge. Then he would hold his arm out, trying to keep it at the same level for a second. If there were things on the counter—junk mail, mother's shed bracelets, restaurant mints—they were swept off in this way. My mother used to stop his hand by putting hers down on his and pressing. For a few moments he moved both their hands along, very slowly, before his fingers lifted up under the weight, like those overloaded donkey carts you sometimes see on dusty streets, held aloft by their burdens.

While on probation, he tried burning down a house with *busy* stained glass windows. The windows depicted a lush jungle scene, and the interior of the house was buried under zebra print, fake palm fronds, and red velvet couches. The owner was the retired principal of my high school. After he left the school, he wore a fresh kimono every day and walked five small, exotic dogs on a complex twisted leash, so it seemed the dogs were leading one another while the line to my old principal was slack. During one of these walks, my dad set the old man's garbage on fire, hoping it would ignite the house, but it only melted the bin part way and made the neighborhood stink.

That's what ugly smells like, he said, paging through an interior design magazine as two policemen clomped up the stairs, joking with each other so boisterously that when I opened the door, false solemnity snatched over their faces like sheets yanked over caught lovers. They hid their snickers with coughing fits as they walked Dad out. For a few days the house was a peaceful place. Without his expansive connoisseurship, the tyranny of taste, I could experience the toaster, switch plates, and spoons without a thought to the missteps or glories of their forms. Mother and I ate off the old flowered china and didn't bother to nicely plate the meal, monograming it with sauce. He always told me I had the worst problem—no taste—worse than even bad taste, since bad taste required *at least a point of view*.

The cube is warm in my hand, and I keep sort of tossing it in front of me as I walk. I've never been a good catch, but I'm catching it fluidly each time. A few people—nannies, mostly—rattle by with strollers, and kids squeal as they spot my game. When I was young, after my father left, my mother dressed me bizarrely for quite some time. For instance, she sometimes had me wear different plaids from head to toe, or found several zippered pieces—pants, shirt, boots—and put them all on me at once. It seemed to be a problem for everyone else but me. Even schoolkids, with their reputation for cruelty, felt compelled to give me gentle tutorials on what looked right, speaking with strong authority about what buttons to leave unbuttoned and the like. When I told Mother this, she grabbed my face, looked me in the eye with unsettling intensity, and told me never to forget the freedom that was ugliness.

My girlfriend Yolanda picks me up by the gate to the development. I lean over to hug her, and she feels the sharp angles of the cube in my palm. She wants to know why I still have the cube; wasn't I supposed to finally say my goodbyes? Yolanda is dressed like always— a skirt and shirt, big jewelry, and her purse, fat like a bladder, quivers by the shifter. It's made of a soft, crinkled leather and resembles, in its general aspect, those old-fashioned cold compresses for headaches. A leather tassel hangs off its side. There is something obscene in the way the purse rests between us—plops, really—opulent, heavy-bellied, and insolent, like some coddled prince of a foreign land. The gray-brown color—a versatile neutral, Yolanda said—is so much like the gelatinous skein of fat at the margins of cheap meat cuts. It is terrible.

The windows are down and the air rushes around us. I hold the cube of my father in one hand. In a sudden motion, I grab the purse with the other and hurl it from the moving car. Yolanda howls. The brakes engage and the car skids to a stop. Yolanda jumps out. I look around, praying this was a fluke. I see the clean-lined road, the nasty brackish ditch water where the purse sinks, the lovely tree canopy, the overstuffed lumps of cumulous clouds. The world cleaves into beautiful and ugly things; it is just as bad as seeing double or hallucinating. I watch as Yolanda pulls the purse out of the ditch gingerly, backing up with it like a collie pulling a drowned toddler from a river. She slips and curses up at me.

I put my head down for a moment and sit in my own dark. For years Mother darkly intimated that I would end up like Dad. She's in Florida now, amongst her ceramic cow figurines, crocheting garish beach totes—hideous objects meant to ward off any tastemaker retirees who might spirit her away. Just a blip, I say to myself, but then I look up and see the shabby-chic glamor of my Yolanda (her skin through the mud like peeling strips of Victorian wallpaper, freckled buds among cream), and I tighten my hold on the cube.

ORNAMENT AND CRIME

113

SNIPPET AND THE RAINBOW BRIDGE

I

A pony hangs from a sling in the middle of a barn aisle in Indiana. His front right cannon bone is broken and in a thick white cast with a slight curve for the knee. He is a silver dun with patches of white on his head and belly and streaking his mane. His name is Snippet, and he is eleven years old and thirteen hands high. His past is unknown, though for a time he was likely owned by the Amish and used as an errand-running horse for the children. At some point he was neglected, and he ended up skeletal and shaking in an auction ring in Shipshewana, Indiana. There he was purchased, for sixty dollars, by Heart's Journey, an equine rescue nonprofit. After he was rehabbed, he became known as the Painting Pony, one of the few horses trained to lift a brush in his mouth, dip it into a bucket of paint, and press it to a large sheet of paper, again and again. Then he broke his leg.

His sling hangs from the rafters at four points, suspending him inches from the aisle floor. He is hooked to an IV that enters the arched muscle of his neck. Beneath him, white sawdust covers the concrete, and a Rubbermaid box filled with antibiotics, Vetrap, bandages, Betadine, bute, etc., is stored off to his right. His water bucket, grain pan, and hay net are propped up in front of him on a wooden cart. The stall doors, off to his right and left, are decorated with get-well cards. Most of these contain his crude likeness, drawn under rainbows or among a funnel cloud of hearts and stars. A few depict him painting, leaning back and dangling the brush from a dexterous hoof. A tinfoil helium balloon that says "Get Well Soon" is tied around the stall bars, and a small herd of stuffed animals is tucked between them. One of Snippet's own paintings—irregular puffs of green, blue, and pink floating over a linear red scrawl—stands on an easel in the pony's view.

It had been Marti's idea to put the painting there. Her thought was that the painting might inspire the pony's healing, remind him of what he needed to get back to. Marti is one-half of Heart's Journey, the founder and CEO. She's the emotive one, the one whose mascara is forever running down her face (why does she even wear it?) as she weeps in empathy over an equine's pain. She's forty-seven, with the rough look of someone with a *past*—drugs, spousal abuse, jail time— all this seems inherent in the cut of her Carharts, the crispy taper of her long hair, the tremulous wrinkles that seem to rotate around her mouth as she speaks in that confidential half-whisper, as if she were in hiding with whoever is listening. She seems threadbare, fragile, ready to break down or apart, yet she is so at home at the edge of ruin that she seems interred there, no closer to destruction than she is from health. She is sitting on a grain sack in the feed room.

Her partner, Judy, is picking up all the medical flotsam that has washed up by the pony, as if he were the shore of a toxic sea. She kicks the dog away from a bloody wad of gauze; she rolls up the Vetrap, combines two nearly empty bottles of iodine. She picks up several syringes and fans them in her hand, as if their needles must be kept apart, then drops them all in the coffee can for sharps. Judy is forty-two; like a twelve-year-old girl left in the elements for thirty years, she is faded, with faint cracks for smile lines, but her childhood form is essentially unchanged, right down to the sloppy long hair and perky joint-floppiness that marks her movement. Unlike Marti, she seems fresh and healthful; she speaks with an insistent but soft voice, as if she knew her good common sense is disruptive enough and aims to dampen its inherent blows. Often she is the one pulling friends and family back from excess or irrationality; she is that steadying hand on your shoulder before you do something rash. She cleans up around the pony and whistles in a strained and breathy way, like someone who has never really learned how. The barn is very quiet, apart from the padding of the dogs, the sighs and shifts of the pony, and the occasional plop of loose stool from him, which hits the aisle with a wet hiss.

II

Two vets are heading toward Heart's Journey. One is Dr. Jim, from Coldwater, a sixty-year-old large-animal vet who graduated from the land-grant college way back. He is extremely tall, with a concave thinness, like a sail full of wind. His hair is mostly white and his face has a grim, angular look whenever he is serious, which he rarely is. Most often, he's making smooth, small jokes to put people—taciturn farmers, waitresses, strangers waiting in a long line at the bank—at ease. He climbs into his truck adorned with the faded decal of a longhorn (though there are none in the area), turns the key, and smiles when an old George Jones song comes on. In the back of the truck, a canister of bull semen bounces like an antsy child as he eases over the dirt roads. He had to leave his dinner for this call, push his chair away from the peach cobbler and pull on his boots. As he laced up all the eyelets, his wife wrapped his pie slice in tinfoil and asked where he was going. "To see to the crazy ladies' horses," he said, and she nodded. She was never in the habit of asking further questions.

Dr. Jim drives by several farms he does business with—the Skitema dairy, the Yoder's pig operation, and a smattering of small farms and 4-Hers he seasonally visits. It is a cool day for early September, and the clumped beef cattle in the field resemble a large dark hand softly gripping the hilltop, like a father steering a toddler by the head. He needs to drop the semen off there on his way back from Heart's Journey. Out of the rabbit hole and onto solid ground. Heart's Journey—

with its silly hand-painted sign, water troughs full of organic herbs and flowers, horses limping around the fields, and pair of unmarried hippie owners—was about as far from John Lidden's beef operation as you could get. Two women staggering around in rose-colored glasses, believing every beat-to-hell old horse farted rainbows. Still, there was something he liked about the place in spite of himself.

III

Dr. Merrill is also on his way to Heart's Journey. He is forty-nine years old and the lead veterinarian at EquiPerformance LLC. He rarely makes farm calls these days, and his assistant, Susan, seems startled when he says where he's heading. Horse owners usually come to the clinic, driving up in diamond-chromed gooseneck rigs with matching trucks. On most days, a fancy horse—a dressage warmblood, a jumper, a quarter horse reiner so muscled and slick it looks like rumpled silk—would trot on the pavement strip while he squinted to see any syncopation in the gait. Even when the irregularity was imperceptible, the owners would want a full workup. Dr. Merrill would snap the films up onto the lighted wall, gesturing at the blurred margin of a tendon, the slightly abnormal angle of a coffin bone, the compressed space in a joint capsule. Many of his cases involve vague complaints that sap a performance horse's brilliance: a short stride, a stiff jump, a sticky turn, all well short of an actual limp.

He instills hope in horse owners by hunkering down a bit, like a chummy waiter, and offering up a menu of edgy treatments: shockwave, stem-cell, Aquatred, etc. He reminds his clients that there are options—there are almost always options, things to try—and his looks seem to second him. His eyes are wide set and show a lot of very bright white, so his hazel irises appear to be sinking in milk. This babyish feature is undercut by a bunched brow, as if his eyes were pulling toward each other, like drops of water on a tabletop laboring to flow together. His hair is youthfully tousled, his neck is loose, his ears are tight and thinly veined as buds. His form is hard and thin, giving the sense of having been whittled away from something larger.

Heart's Journey is few towns away, and Dr. Merrill merges onto the highway. The landscape is so bleary and overcast that the road seems hyperreal. It reminds him of bad cartoons, where the main characters and scenes are crisp and bright, while everything beyond is summed up in a few gesturing lines. Still, he is glad to push off the day's appointments. And the idea of the scruffy barn dogs and tame chickens swarming about his legs sounds nice, right about now. He'll show them, today, that he remembers their names. The bantam, for instance, is Oscar ...

IV

It says something about you, the vet you choose. Early on, the two women chose vets like spouses choose sides of beds. They needed a vet almost monthly—for routine shots and for the problems rescue horses usually brought with them. Marti preferred Dr. Merrill— a vet who seemed a connoisseur of equine pain, able to treat it, she thought, because he knew all its guises. When he recommended a course of treatment, he spoke in a low, emphatic voice, full of caution and caveats, as if he were revealing some difficult private knowledge. It was that sense of painful confession, married with his intense bedside manner, that made Marti feel at home.

For Judy, it was Dr. Jim, the cutup country vet with the habit of slapping the horses' hindquarters like a car hood when he was done with them. He blurted out his diagnoses and waved his hands whenever the women asked for more specifics, as if details were an indulgence he was withholding for their own good. The particularly sorry cases— the really broken down horses—he had little patience for. "Best to let them move along," he said, his euphemism for euthanasia, as if they were already passing by on a conveyer. There was something honest, Judy thought, in his refusal to get caught up in anything murky.

Inevitably, both women see a character flaw made manifest in the other woman's vet preference. Marti can see that, despite her practical airs, Judy is afraid to delve into real troubles, to live with unknown outcomes. Judy, watching Marti and Dr. Merrill speak nearly cheek to cheek over some sketchy diagnostic, sees a woman who needs coddling, who relishes the minutiae of sickness under the guise of trying to heal it.

v

Over the barn, there is a bridge, a large bright-banded arch, as noxious as corporate branding bandied about in a boardroom. The bridge is self-contained; it is like a piece of garden décor that can be repositioned wherever it looks best; it performs no function other than to imitate a bridge, to give a sense of crossing. This is the Rainbow Bridge, and it is referenced often by Marti and Judy as if it were as solid as the feed store down the road. The Rainbow Bridge is animal rescuer parlance for the interfaith zone where dead animals go, the sphere where old, unsteady horses are restored to an eternal youth. Pet dogs who lived in different decades and never crossed paths on earth snort each other's buttocks in the sky. Cats cash in their unused lives for cloud perches near the sun. Or some such thing.

The Bridge comes up between the women with some regularity. They've kept horses from it and sent horses to it. They've pulled horses off slaughter trucks, they've outbid the kill-buyers at Shipshewana, they've carefully rehabbed starvation cases and neglect cases, calling the farrier in to trim the long, curled hoofs, like elfin slippers, on some of the worst. They've also had to put a fair number of horses down—Raven, with the ulcerated, cancerous eye; Henry, with the inoperable colic; the deformed colt Jet, who walked on his pasterns; the old mare Olena, whose ringbone and navicular kept her down so long she developed bedsores. Then there was Yankee, the off-track Thoroughbred who twice flipped over under tack, nearly killing Marti. A particularly troubling case, as he was young and beautiful and completely deadly—

VI

Before he left the office for Heart's Journey, Dr. Merrill had asked Susan to cancel his appointment with his client Deborah and her mare, Luna. Luna is lame again, this time in the hind end. Before, it was the left fetlock. Before that, a string of abscesses kept her out of commission for the better part of six months. Before that, she bowed a tendon. Before that, she popped a splint. There is another before that, but Dr. Merrill likes to pretend the mare has just appeared to him, in the hopes that he can view her present problem, whatever it is, with fresh eyes. The mare is tall and chestnut, with an excessive femininity to her face—long lashes, big, quivery eyes, fine ears, and a buttery muzzle. Deborah has the same kind of look, with jutting plump lips that seem to tussle, as if playfully trying to mount one another. She listens to Dr. Merrill and nods her head. Sometimes she voices a doubt—would Luna ever be right?—and blushes. *Of course*, Dr. Merrill answers, and Deborah goes brighter and looks down, as if her question were evidence of a small-minded faithlessness and not a reasonable question, considering. Then they move on to the next treatment. This has gone on for almost six years. Nothing in Luna's radiographs, X-rays, bone scans, ultrasounds, or blood panels has ever indicated anything beyond minor problems and good prognoses, so he never tells Deborah bad news. Nothing that has been wrong with the mare is unfixable, so he fixes each thing. But the mare will not stay sound. After two months of being ridden, she's dragging a toe around turns. Deborah too ages over these six years. He watches her ripen, then go oversweet on the vine. The lips get dewier, the eyes mistier, the clothing brighter, the figure fuller, so that during a certain appointment—perhaps when they injected the mare's hocks—Deborah is glaringly lovely, a nearly painful concentration of beauty. Seeing her makes his teeth hurt, as if biting into something too rich. He concentrates on her shoes—soft leather ankle boots, ill-suited to a barn—and sends her on her way with a breezy, encouraging comment: he hopes to see neither of them again soon. The next time he sees them, or the time after that, Deborah's skin is heavier. The red waves of her hair are dry and compressed into a clip on top of her head, like leaves flattened in a compost bag. The large, wet mouth on the slackened face looks pathological, seductiveness flaring like a growth. The horse still stands at the end of its rope and blinks its fawn eyes, then limps its little limp as Deborah leads her into a jog. She stops the horse and looks at Dr. Merrill with the shamed-hopeful look of a kid pulling back panty elastic to give a glimpse to a playground pal—*I dare you to say it's okay*. He pats her back. They bend over readouts and share breath. Assistants shuffle in the hall; he sees the shadowy blips of their shoes under the door, like flickering ellipses. Even as he murmurs assurances he stares at the image, feeling, not for the first time, that it is secretly enchanted, like those joke portraits whose eyes move as you walk by. The image is pristine, textbook; the lesions and edemas blink into view the minute he looks away. The horse is healthy. The horse is not well. Deborah smells gamy; he finds himself rubbing her hair absently, like he would a horse. Just a small problem, here, that's all.

Yes, good to get away.

VII

Judy wants to be blue. Everything in her midst seems blue. There's blue print on the bottle of bute. There's a blue plush goat in the stall bars, and the Vetrap securing the fraying bottom of Snippet's cast is blue. The sky outside the open barn doors, though it had been overcast for a week, is now a shocking shade of azure, bright even where the sun is not. Even the gray tomcat, who caterwauls high in the hayloft, looks bluish as he flicks his tail over a bar of light reaching through the eaves.

Judy had taken the True Colors personality assessment earlier that week; it had been free for the heads of local businesses (*I run a nonprofit,* she'd said). She was sure she'd be a blue (caring, creative, intuitive), but instead the results of the test had pegged her a green (analytical, logical, emotionally detached), and although the facilitators made clear there were "no bad colors," Judy knew all she needed to know from the other greens she'd been grouped with.

To her left, a Realtor woman with a drippy spray tan complained about the buzz of the fluorescent lights. To her right, the owner of a cheese shop droned on about her warring skin diseases, how one rash actually healed the other, oblivious to the discomfort of her listeners. Judy looked at the blue group across the room. They clustered around their table like bright birds at a birdbath, tittering with excitement, stretching up to flutter their colors—one woman bounced in her chair, her red hair in a chignon like a curled feather. They laughed, they spoke earnestly and quickly; to Judy they looked like artists transported from an earlier age, writers in a jazz club. I used to be that way, she thought. What happened?

Snippet is dozing, jerking in his sleep. The tips of his suspended hooves scrape the pavement, throwing off sparks. Judy puts her hand under his thick striped mane. She lays her face against his neck, feeling his long guard hairs, the vestiges of his winter coat that would have been fully shed if he were able to roll in the sand or if he were up to being curried. But he is a horse that hates being brushed, hates typical gestures of affection, and normally Judy's proximity would have caused him to dance sidewise, to perhaps nip at her coat, to roll his large black eye so the white sclera showed, so that he looked skeptical and affronted, although Judy always got the sense it was a put-on and that Snippet merely liked to play with expectations.

Which was why, when your back was to him, he would sometimes put his muzzle on your shoulder and nibble very lightly. But when you turned around, he'd gallop off with a squeal, so you were left wondering at his intent: was the closeness the point, and the wheeling away just a way to maintain his toughness, a kind of embarrassed backpedaling? Or was the wheeling away the point, and the moment of closeness just a joke, just a commentary on how willing you were to believe in his affection, how vulnerable and dense you were?

VIII

Dr. Jim is a few miles from Heart's Journey. He's turned the radio off. He's thinking of the pony's radiographs and following what he considers to be a foolish train of thought. He doesn't look at many X-rays in his practice, and he felt bizarrely charmed when he slid them out of the mailer the other day. The pony's cannon bone—split white against the gray fuzz of the surrounding tissue—looked to him like a thin woman in a white shift, turning away from the camera. A high, small bone chip appeared to be the barest suggestion of a fine upturned nose, lost in the angling of her cheek. An oddly romantic image, like a frame of film from an old silent picture.

Of course he would recommend euthanasia—nothing else made sense. The pony was just a pet, but his advice would be the same even if it were a pricey herd bull. He has his kit with him and is prepared to put the pony down on the spot.

He drives slower and slower. The dirt roads, at dinnertime, are nearly empty, and his truck crawls. The films are in a sleeve on his passenger side. He reaches over and taps them out, idly, as if by accident. The image slides out. The woman, again. The crack in the bone is like a sash at her waist. What if he tried to fix the pony? His friends, the cattlemen, would rib him at the diner. They'd laugh and say he'd gone soft in the head, give him shit about retiring. His wife would shake her head in amusement or dismissal, he wouldn't know. His young son would bark a laugh, bits of sausage and milk spritzing the table cloth.

The break is open, but the bony column was aligned. The pony is small—five hundred pounds—that is key. What about a weight-bearing cast with longitudinal support? A sort of standing splint? He stops the truck and feels behind his seat. He lays the tire iron on the radiograph.

IX

Marti is in the feed room. The bag she sits on bulges and kernels work their way out of the plastic weave. Mumu, the obese calico, is curled on another bag, kneading and purring, rolling her head around, wishing to be touched. Marti wants a cigarette, but she quit. She wants a drink, but she quit that, too. She wants to leave the barn and go to Rosco's, dance with Jim, argue with the bartender, drive by the street she used to live on, write a letter to her first foster family, smoke a joint, shout at someone, try on a dress for someone, sleep on a floor, wake up someplace else, but she quit all that, too.

She's always had a lot of wants. It used to be she felt all of them, the way you feel each staggered drop when it begins to rain. Then they became a weather, nothing to blink at.

With a piece of hay she digs at the crescents of dirt under her fingernails. She hears Snippet struggle in the sling and Judy's voice quieting him. She should go out there and help her, discuss what should be done with the pony, but she doesn't feel up to it.

She squeezes her eyes shut and watches the pops of yellow and red, the light show playing in the dark. Those flashes of light—ghosts of light she'd seen, no doubt, the shapes of lamplight and bare bulbs

like a visual echo—she bore down on them as if they were conceal-
ing something. They were bright shards of someplace else, she always
thought as a kid, evidence of another world peeping through. Her
stepfather once pushed her down and she hit her head on a planter.
Her ears hummed and the light she saw was varied and streaky, as if
she were being drawn through a nighttime cityscape on the back of a
speeding motorcycle. It wasn't heavenly or spiritual—it lacked the solemnity—but wildly festive. It seemed more real than her stepfather
or the push; both the man and the act struck her as chintzy in com-
parison, no longer substantial enough to fear. Even as he bent over
her and begged her to be okay, rocking and holding her hand, she
wondered if he knew he was barely there.

A chicken wanders into the feed room, moving to the beat of its
clucks, turning its head and giving her a deeply skeptical look, its ruff
of red-gold feathers fissuring as it drops its head to peck at the floor.
Marti reaches down and brushes her fingers over his comb; it feels to
her like the hand of a limp doll.

X

The thing he had to do, he knew, was to cut Deborah off. Tell her that,
given Luna's long history of problems, she was probably just prone
to unsoundness, and the best thing would be to make her a brood
mare or a pasture pet. Just cut it off. The whole thing kept shaking
him up. Sometimes he came home so distracted that his wife and son
seemed to be just so much subclinical white noise, a side project he'd
unwisely taken on. Laura would ask him what was wrong, looping her
arms around his neck. All he could manage to say was that his mind
was on a "hard case."

He couldn't tell her about Luna—he was loath to admit his obsession with the case, the lack of progress. There were far more dramatic
cases that he could have on his mind, cases he did tell Laura about—

a dicey colic surgery on a big-time jumper, a de-gloved pastern freed from barbed wire, barely salvaged, a breech birth unable to be righted. And of course he told her about Snippet, the miniscule pony with the catastrophically shattered leg.

"Is that the one who paints?" she'd said, and he'd looked at her blankly before remembering that yes, the two women had taught the pony to slop paint around. He and Laura had been watching the news when a local interest story on Snippet and Heart's Journey came on. In the clip, Judy and Marti handed a brush to the pony, who took it in his teeth then flung his head up and down, like an athlete making theater out of working a kink out of his neck. Paint spritzed on the women and the newscaster, an effusive woman with a smile so high and wide it showed all her gums, as if her upper lip were the corner of a yogurt lid, there for ease of peeling.

"That pony's hilarious," Laura remarked. She was in fact eating a yogurt on the couch next to him—she was always watching her weight and working out—and her trimness had a parched, vacuum-packed quality, like a foodstuff that would need reconstituting with water to be palatable. His attraction to her had dribbled away as his practice became more consuming, but it struck him not as a loss but as a practical shift, the way you might rehab a horse with sore front heels by developing the carrying power of his hocks and hind end.

On the TV, Snippet was creating a swirl of blotchy colors, his tail a counterweight to the brush, swishing left when he made a right stroke, flagging when he dropped his head and stabbed at the bottom of the canvas. The camera flicked to Marti and Judy, who looked especially eccentric in the studio lights; even with the camera makeup and hair they looked like drifters, gaping at some rare vision unfolding down by the overpass.

The donkey farm on his right tells him he's a mile or so out from Heart's Journey. Snippet hadn't been responding well to the soft cast and the sling, so the next step, if there was a next step, would be a table surgery and then a long, long rehab—at least a year, with much of that time tranquillized to prevent him from thrashing around and blowing out the pins from his bones. A twenty percent chance of recovery, if that. Normally he'd go for it if they would—which they would, at least if the same woman—was it Martina?—was at the helm. He recalled a hushed conversation with her in the tack room; her swimmy eyes searching his, translating all his nuance into two words: hope or hopeless.

He cringes at the thought of it—another vortex. He ought to just recommend euthanasia and be done with it. The afternoon sun moves through the cab of his truck like a hand feeling for something lost. It sets on the chrome details of his bag, where two files are tucked away—one for Snippet and one for Luna. If he puts Snippet down to-day—or just gives his recommendation and leaves—he can get back to the office and perhaps Deborah can come to a later appointment. There, he will let her know . . .

Dr. Merrill looks at his bag, the tongue of light on the left handle. Luna's latest radiograph flicks across his mind unbidden, like it often does. The black and grey fuzz of the image seems to crackle and squirm in his thoughts, as if he were in the process of tuning it in, moving rabbit ears to catch a signal that floats enticingly near. Something in the angle of the pedal bone? . . . not that it matters. No harm, though, in looking at the radiograph one more time, just to confirm.

XI

The problem is Marti. Being around that woman had changed her, made her harder, turned her green. Marti is so delicate, so emotional, that Judy has had to be strong and coldly logical just to keep some semblance of order around the farm. Marti's whole personality is like a sculpture Judy once saw of small, very thin reeds fed into each other to make a latticework so fragile it had to be protected from even the breath of the gallery-goers. It was in a glass case, in shadow, since light would degrade the organic material. Judy spent a long time staring at it, trying to figure out what, exactly, was holding it up. It was half-collapsed, so how . . . ? She'd looked at her program. *The integrity of the piece depends on the forces of gravity bearing down; it gathers strength as it falls into itself . . .*

Judy always has to do the dirty work: to turn away a horse from the rescue (otherwise they'd become hoarders—something Marti certainly was before Judy came on board), to cease treatment of a too-far-gone horse, to make the call to send a horse to the Rainbow Bridge, to hold the horse's lead rope while the vet administered the shot. How many lead ropes had she held in this way? How many times did she gently tug down on the rope, encouraging the horse, even as he blinked out of existence, to fold his front legs so he would settle down gracefully, rather than simply fall onto his side, convulsing and struggling, far from the peaceful send-off everyone wanted? And in these cases—when the horse left violently, messily, sometimes banging himself in the head, spraying blood through a smashed nasal cavity—how many times had she wanted someone there to comfort her? She wants to tell Marti about these times—Marti should at least hear it—but she doesn't.

There is something about Marti that forces a person to tread carefully. She seems flayed, like some sort of raw nerve flailing around in the world, and her pain seems elevated, deeper, more keenly and destructively felt. It is actually less painful, for Judy, to keep a sad image to herself than to risk Marti becoming upset. It is a kind of power, Judy thinks, to be so vulnerable. Sometimes she wonders if it's a kind of manipulation, too.

For once, Judy thinks, I want to be the irrational one. I'll be the one who can't let go. I'll call that wack-job Dr. Merrill for once. I'll keep Snippet going; I'll throw the rescue's money at him. We'll do surgery. Surgeries. Why not? He's a great pony. Why can't I lose my shit for once?

She wants to return to the illogic at the base of the enterprise, when they stood among all kill buyers, the slaughter-truck drivers, the farmers with the Skoal-can circles on their back pockets, the married Amish men with their heavy beards, gravely nodding, as if speech itself were too newfangled. The auctioneer, all chin and bald head, compresses and fans out his syllables in a showboating blurt, like a shuffler making an arc of his cards. And then, without even looking at Judy, Marti raises her hand. The auctioneer eyes her and nods. The men turn their heads and take her in: her stained Carharts, her long blond hair, the hardship-scored face with the stunned child-eyes. Some laugh, some grumble. The two women pull their pony—hip #467—from the pen. He is so thin and his coat so poor that he looks like a rug remnant tossed over a wrought-iron fence. His forelock is stiff with cockleburs and stands straight up like a plume; despite his condition he wears it that way, like he knows he is something to see. The two women lead him out, whooping and laughing, giddy with the absurdity of what they've taken on.

XII

The last time he'd fashioned a medical device he used a bamboo flute and a ripped shirt. The solider was in so much pain he'd bit a hole in his lip. He pressed the flute to the boy's shin, tore up his undershirt, wrapped it around and held the excess in his teeth to keep the tension, then tied it off. "Don't run off or your leg will whistle." Dr. Jim never joked crudely, nor swore, nor made coarse comments about women, nor employed gallows humor. He was an oddity in the barracks, and while the other men made fun of him often (his nickname was Norman Rockwell), they saw the resilience and subversion in his simple sunny jokes. "Goddamn you, Rockwell," the boy had said, grimacing as Dr. Jim pulled him to his feet.

When he makes a comment to cut the tension, he likes to watch how it falls on the atmosphere, much like a golfer shades his eyes and traces the trajectory of his shot. The tense, silent people at the bank, for instance, ripple and shift, rolling their eyes, chuckling or smiling tightly. These slight movements break up the scene suddenly and dramatically; it is like a shattered pane of glass finally buckling into millions of shards. They can no longer be a line of silent strangers.

He is joking with himself, these thoughts of trying to fix the pony. He'd have to make this drive over and over to work on the patient. Probably he would work in a haze of incense, Marti or Judy (he never remembered who was who) would talk to him about the pony's feelings and thoughts, he would be made to contemplate the pony's paintings, and the pony itself would wobble around, comically debased in the walking cast he'd cook up in his basement shop. He looks at the film again. He thinks of the simplicity of the splint, how easy it would be to try. The look of the cattlemen when they found out.

XIII

The aisle is quiet and Marti ventures out. Judy is out riding the Gator, tossing flakes of hay over the pasture fences while the horses gallop around. Snippet dozes, the white Medicine Hat marking over his ears bright in the afternoon light, like a fresh doily on a worn couch. She pats him, studies one of his paintings, his last before the accident. Most of his paintings were sloppy, flung over the whole canvas and beyond, but this one is comprised of just a few frilly disks of paint, pressed over each other, as symmetrical as if it had been made with a spirograph. It looks familiar, somehow, and then she remembers where she'd seen something like it before.

Marti's foster mother, Gwen, used to wear a silk flower like that, every day, pinned to her headband, her scarves, or the hem of her shorts if it was hot out. It was blue and green and cheaply made with a fake pearl in the center, but Gwen never went without it. Once, Marti had gotten lost in an outdoor market, a swirling place chockful with wares of all kinds: herbs, blown glass, collectible pins, handmade clothes. She'd wandered away from Gwen to look at a table covered with tumbled stones. The man explained the powers of each one: the bright flecks in the pyrite refreshed one's courage, while rosy quartz, held to one's temple, could catch the thoughts of others and refract them into your head. He leaned over the table, took her by her wrist, and tried to place a magnetic bracelet on her. His grip was wet, his eyes pink rimmed, and a winter hat with a leaping deer was pulled low on his gray head even though it was June. She jerked back and realized Gwen was nowhere in sight.

In the haze and heat she walked, looking for her foster mother, trying not to walk in circles, though she kept seeing the same blond women and their clumps of reed baskets swaying in the sun. She looked for Gwen's feet in their simple Greek sandals, or her streaming scarves, but there were many scarves and feet. Panic hit her. She had the awful feeling that this market was the whole of her existence and she'd be walking by these glass unicorns and bowls of beads forever. But then she saw, through the indeterminate mix of bare legs and colors, Gwen's perpetual flower. She saw it long before she saw Gwen, as if the flower were a prick of light that opened to reveal her, its petals an aperture.

She hasn't thought about Gwen in a long time. The flower's appearance on the canvas again suggested a keyhole to another place, and she remembers that Gwen used to say that she was an indigo child, possessed of a heightened vision and aura. No one else said that about her, so when Gwen got sick and Marti was moved to a new home, she tried to forget it. Auras and visions would not have played well in her second home, that was for sure.

She puts a hand on the painting and a hand on Snippet's sleeping forehead. She shuts her eyes. A tingle runs through her like a thread; it felt irritatingly minute, like a hair in your mouth. Gwen always talked about the inner eye, how it opened, blinked, and fluttered in response to the vibrations of emotions. Hers had snapped open. Snippet wants to go, she thinks. He wants to slip into the opening he made and enter the new place. She would call Dr. Jim, make herself hold the rope for once, and see.

XIV

To live in a horse's body is to experience a perpetual loop of sensation, as if each nerve ending were being plucked in a pattern. Sometimes the patterns change or stutter: this is thought. Normally you feel the hair at the base of your tail twice, then the inside of your esophagus; now the order is switched, and that has meaning. Then, of course, there are the eyes, set on the side of the head. It is like being at a themed ride at an amusement park: everything to the side is thrilling and bright, but the area right in front of the car is black. Your world is peripheral. The blind spot in the center of your vision is your center, dark and certain, a void you can retreat to whenever you want. Sometimes the people and buildings and grass and pasture fold over you and push you into that center, like a stone held secret in a fist. At these times, your sovereignty becomes a question, a source of suspicion, a mystery. People holler at you and peer in your eyes with a bright light, trying to see if you are still there.

THE CHAUTAUQUA SESSIONS

My son, the drug addict, is about to tell a story. I can tell because he's closed his eyes and lifted his chin. I can tell because he's laid his hands, palms down, on the table, like a shaman feeling the energy of the tree-spirit still in the wood. I can tell because he's drawing a shuddering breath, as if what he has to say will take all he's got. He's putting on the full show because he has a new audience—he'd streamline the theatrics if it were only me. We're having dinner in Levi Lambright's recording compound, Chautauqua, in remote Appalachian Tennessee. I'm a songwriter—a lyricist—and I'm here to work on a new album with Levi, our first in fifteen years. Dee was not invited. The only other person who should be here is Lucinda, Levi's cook. But Dee just showed up, the way drug-addicted sons sometimes do.

Right as he's about to speak, I reach for the wine bottle and refill my glass, placing the bottle back down in front of me, providing a bit of a visual shield between us. He's sitting across from me, next to Levi. The kid looks good, I'll give him that. He's clean shaven, and his dun-colored hair appears professionally cut. His eyes, where the cresting chaos can most often be seen, are clear and still. They still don't track exactly right, though. Like his mother, he looks at you out of one eye at a time, like a quizzical parrot. If you look at him straight on, his thin face seems to wobble and shake like a coin on end before it flips back into profile, his mother's aquiline nose and sharp chin etched in the center of his round boy's head. On his forearm, his old self-mutilation scars have been scribbled over, I see, with a new homemade tattoo: *Trust.* I don't see myself in him at all.

"Okay? Are you sure you want to hear this? It's kind of a long story." Dee asks, though he doesn't pause before going on.

"This happened last week. I was downtown, on some crazy uppers. I think I took some MDMA that night. Maybe just amphetamines. I don't remember. All I know is I was high, really high, and I'd been dancing and couldn't find who I came with. So I decide I should go home. But when I leave the club, I can't figure out where I am. I mean, I only live a block from there. I'm walking down the street and I feel like I'm in a foreign country or something. Nothing is familiar. Somehow I ended up three miles away, in the worst part of town . . ."

I try not to listen. I've heard all this before, and I'm pretty sure it will end with him confronting the godhead. I've gotten enough midnight calls about his drug-fueled encounters with an encyclopedic list of spiritual figures: Jesus, Buddha, Allah, The Spirit in the Sky, and Mother Nature herself, who held out long arms made of saplings and drew him to her leafy bosom while nibbling a Morse code of secret truth on his earlobe. As much as I knew the source of these visions, it was hard not to be swept along by his telling. Because Dee got one thing from me: my ability to spin a story.

Sometimes Dee's language was so striking during these soliloquies that I would find myself jotting down phrases without thinking. *I can't believe you mined your drugged son for a good turn of phrase*, I'd think, looking down at the pad the next morning. Then, a preposterous jealously: *Why can't I think of phrases like that?* I'd want to use the words in my work, but that seemed somehow wrong, given what they sprang from. But to let that language, no matter how destructive its origin, simply be forgotten seemed wrong, too. So I simply recorded it on little sheets of notepaper that I stored in a shoebox under my bed. I guess I figured I'd decide what to do with it all someday. I suppose it's a bit like the newspaper clippings proud parents keep of their kids' accomplishments, for they were, in their perverse way, Dee's accomplishments.

"Man, have I been there!" Levi is staring at my son, a smile playing about his lips as though he knows he's going to hear something great. He looks at me and gestures with his fork, flinging bits of food into his drink. "Danny, remember when the tour bus got lost on the way to Santa Fe? And how we hopped out and started looking for street signs and ended up at that crazy pueblo with those cult people? The ones with all the chickens wearing stuff?"

I nod. I remember the chickens and their colorful neck warmers, scratching around in the sand while a few children sat in the sun with looms on their knees. They'd looked at the group of us—back then Levi was a bona fide rock star—with a somnolent disinterest, as if we were deeply beside the point. There's more to the story, but I don't want to tell it with Dee here. It's a funny story, and telling a funny story is an act of generosity and welcome that I certainly don't feel.

"So you were stoned and lost. And . . . ?"

Dee fixes his left eye on me and then flips his hands upward in an emphatic gesture. There's a faint purplish streak coming off his tear duct and down his cheek, like a magic marker he's tried to wash off. His inner elbow is blotchy with thick pancake makeup, but track marks peek through like the bubbles of crabs submerged in wet sand. He leans over the table, as close to me as he can get.

"I brought a man back to *life*. That's what happened."

Only one of my two sons Dale is a druggie. That's right: I have two sons by the same name—the absurd result of a tanking romance. That's why this Dale goes by Dee. He's the younger one—just twenty-four—the son of my second ex-wife, whose love for me primarily manifested itself in an intense jealously of my first wife, Gina. Vicki had the notion that she was simply a placeholder for that old passion. This was hardly the case—far from being a woman I pined for, Gina had morphed, for me, into the kind of pleasant asexuality that one associates with kin of the fun-cousin variety. I tried to make that clear, but simply hearing Gina's name on my tongue was all it took to send

Vicki off the edge. "Listen to the way you make love to the very syllables!" It came to a head when she was pregnant with our son. "I want
to name him Dale," she told me over dinner, a wine glass half-filled
with grape juice shaking in her hand. "But Vicki, I already have a ten-
year-old son by that name," I said slowly, as if to a child. "Gina's son,"
was all she said in reply. I gave in, figuring that naming my second son
the same name as my first was such an extreme testimony to my love
for her that it would cure her jealousy for good. But within a few years
I had not only another Dale, but another ex-wife.

After the divorce, Vicki and Dee moved to Dearborn, where she immediately married a gruff, possessive pharmaceutical salesman who
picked up the phone whenever I called her to discuss our son. So all
the calls—even the later ones where we grimly discussed Dee's drug
problems—were set to her husband's breathing, as if the call were
coming through a conch shell. Weekend handoffs were tense, and I
always felt I was smuggling the boy away as I hustled him to the car
while Vicki and the husband stared through the bay window, blowing
Dee kisses and making theatrical frown-faces. Once Dee and I were
safely on the highway, I'd look over at him—slumped in the passenger
side, his bag on his lap, his watery blue eyes turning in their sockets
with a reptilian jerkiness—and feel as awkward and duty-bound as a
cop entertaining a lost kid while the mother was rounded up.

I'd like to say that it was just Dee's addictions that had cooled me
on him over the years, that had frayed the precious father-son thread.
But there were things in Dee that had bothered me long before he
started using. Even as a little boy, he was always selling himself too
fervidly, selling whatever he cared about. When he was fifteen, it
was Stanley Kubrick's body of work, and I spent many an afternoon
watching him pause *A Clockwork Orange* frame by frame while he
explained the brilliance of the shot—the shifting chiaroscuro that
played against the elegant curve of a kicking foot. By the time Dee was
eighteen, Kubrick was forgotten, and all Dee spoke about was music.
He listened nonstop to what sounded to me like the drippings of a

leaky pipe in an echoing room mixed with a duck call. Dee claimed that the absence of voices and recognizable instruments represented a higher form of music, untainted by human expression. "These sounds are incidental, you know, found sounds," he explained. "Then they're spliced and looped. That's all that's been done to them. Isn't it beautiful?"

I liked that Dee was passionate, even artistic. Unlike my other son Dale—a bakery franchiser whose imagination stretches no further than how to rebrand the cupcake—Dee seemed more like me, a thinker, someone interested in ideas and art. Yet it was hard to really engage with him. His typical response to anything I said was a wave of a hand and a wincing squint, the same gesture one would use when walking into a smoky room. Still, I loved him. I imagined that when he grew up a bit—got out of Vicki's control a bit more, saw more of the world—that he and I would have a fresh shot. The good times we had (racing down the dunes in northern Michigan and splashing into the lake, paging through catalogs of specialized recording equipment, waxing philosophical about the state of pop music) seemed to contain within them the seed of something better, something more solid. I can wait. That's what I told myself.

But Dee's habit ruined whatever fragile relationship we'd been building. He stole from me, screamed at me, punched me, came onto my then-girlfriend's mentally disabled daughter when she was staying with me (a disaster that was only averted because I walked back into the living room in time), and even accused me, during an acid fugue, of abusing him as a child. Of course that was laughably untrue—I'd hardly touched him at all, much less hit him. I'd been raised by a cold, withholding father who demanded dark and silence whenever he got home from work. When I would fix him his drink, I'd place it into his hands with the gentleness of a small spider, its legs no more than filament. I treated Dee with the same delicacy, only touching him lightly, if at all, and when I hugged him I did not even press away the air under his baggy shirt.

Vicki and I did our best for him. We sent him to the top rehab facilities in the state, even an experiential sailing adventure where the organizers likened ducking to avoid the boom to avoiding drugs, and gathering up the lines to organizing one's life and getting a job. I tried everything I could think of or read about—too much to even recall. And Dee would have good days, of course. They always do. He'd show up at my door and apologize. He'd talk in a low, exaggeratedly modulated voice, as if luxuriating in his ability to speak in something other than an accusatory shriek or a paranoid mumble. We'd go somewhere to eat and he'd stare at his plate in wonder, as if his reentry into the world had given even his limp house salad a kind of sheen. Being with him as he reentered regular life, watching him acquaint himself with all of life's serene pleasures, was bracing and thrilling. It made the world feel new to me. All he'd said and done shed off me like it was nothing. And then—relapse.

Before Tonya, my ex-girlfriend, decided she'd had enough of me, she told me that my willingness to ride the rollercoaster of Dee's deceit, lies, and false recovery so many times was an addiction in itself. "What do you do all day? Read books about recovery. Call his phone constantly. Drive around town looking for him. All for a kid who pretends to be clean once a week, like clockwork, usually to get some money out of you. This kid will get better, or he won't. It can't be on you forever."

She was right. I'd been living off dwindling royalties from my career with Levi, refusing new songwriting work, even from artists I once desperately courted. There was no time for friends. I never bothered to see my other son, even though he lives only a few hours away. And the rooftop community garden, where I had once so enthusiastically volunteered, had taken me off its work schedule since I'd been a no-show too many times, times when I drove right by the garden to hunt down Dee, parking my car by a dark overpass or barren lot, leaping out with a flashlight and calling out his name, raking the light over the faces of those bums and strays he ran with. Each face was lit with a chemically restored naïveté, so even the roughest slow-grinned like toddlers caught in the act of scrawling on the nursery walls. I'd grabbed one I'd seen before—a man who always wore brass-buckled pilgrim shoes and drank from a horn flask—and demanded to know where Dee was. He cocked his head and called out "dee*dee*dee," a sound that rose, echoed, and converged with the faraway car alarms, bird calls, and every other ambient long *e* in the city. Dee was lost and unavoidable. I'd find him dead one day, I thought, or get killed looking for him. There's no other way it could end.

But that, thank god, is all in the past now. Five years down the rabbit hole was plenty. I no longer let myself get involved. I've let myself mourn. I've started working at the garden again, dating a woman named Natalie who knows only the basics about Dee—druggie son, liar, a sad part of my past, a toxic person, if he calls hang up. I'm even ready, now, to write again, something that was impossible when I was involved with Dee's dramas. That's why I'm here. I want to make music again with my old partner—it's time to return to who I was before Dee. Levi has been calling me on and off over the past five years, trying to entice me to write another album. He must have been surprised when I called him and finally agreed. If Levi found out about Dee, I thought, it would be through the songs I'd write.

Dee is well into his story now. He's telling us about wandering into a neighborhood he's never been in before, still lost, still looking for his apartment. It's a bad part of town—and bad for Detroit is plenty bad—and everyone in this neighborhood is squatting in vacated homes. No one owns anything. He enters an old church. The stained glass windows are all broken. Lead solder seams that once marked out the profiles of saints now snake through open space. Someone's painted a mural of a pastoral scene on the bare lath—probably an artist trying to bring a bit of beauty, or just intention, to a place marked by ruin and randomness. Dee walks straight into the wall, thinking he's mounting a velvety hillock. He passes clusters of gang members who ignore him out of sheer surprise, the way a cat will back away from an approaching mouse, as if out of respect for the depth of its suicidal impulse. He stumbles into a huge plastic bag filled with pop cans dragged by an elderly lady riding a Hoveround stamped with the logo of a long-closed supermarket. "There was nothing keeping me going," Dee explains, "but the thought of 'getting home,' which itself, repeated in my head, was basically just a mindless chant. You know, how your name sounds if you repeat it too much? Not only does it not seem like 'you,' it doesn't seem like anything. It seems to just erase more of you the more you say it."

Lucinda makes small, sweet little coos of sympathy with regularity. Levi's two silent, sphinxlike dogs pad in and lower into the sentry position by our chairs, their legs folding under with a perfect, luxurious grace, like the smooth mechanism of a fine pocketknife. Levi's chin is cupped in his hands as he nods along to Dee's words. It's shocking how little Levi has changed over the years. His face is still handsome, just blurred at its edges, his jaw softened in flesh. This does not make him look old but rather uncontained, a face rimmed by a diffuse halo of skin. The skin under Levi's eyes, unlike mine, is pristine and glowing, bright as if someone had dropped a tea light in his empty head. And he's maintained his general expression—the familiar empathy and knowingness that used to make me feel both understood and insubstantial, as if the largesse of his person were being wasted by turning its focus on me.

"Then I walk past these screaming people. Someone grabs my shirt. I think I'm about to be mugged, but I can't get away. It's like I'm moving underwater and everyone else is on dry land . . ."

The story is reaching its climax, I can feel it. The drugs, it seems, have impaired everything in Dee but his grasp of the story arc. A bathroom break might spare me the triumphant rise of Dee's voice, the careen into lyricism. I get up without a backward glance, although I can hear Dee taking a breath, the silverware clinking again, attention turning to the dogs. The bathroom is down a hall so wide that it seems like another room. This whole place is cavernous, open-plan: cathedral ceilings, massive reclaimed wood beams hung with art prints. There are a few framed gold and platinum records on the wall and a picture of Levi and me in the early seventies, both of our feet propped up on a rock, the guitar resting between us. I had a kind of sleepy-eyed shy smile, a look that spoke of both bliss and nerves—Levi's talent intimidated me then, though I was thrilled to be part of it. Those feelings seem so long ago, and I doubt if I ever have that look on my face anymore. Maybe expressions rotate out of a person's face for good, like a song dropped from a set list.

I splash water on my face and try to clear my head. When I turn off the sink, someone's ring slides off the basin and pings around the bowl. It's a little silver seahorse, curving around to touch its snout to its swirled tail. I slip it in my pocket, since I don't want to leave it out for Dee to lift. It's late and Levi's already invited him to stay the night, but he'll be gone tomorrow morning—I'll make sure of it. No reason to worry. But why show up now? Here? I haven't seen him in a year or heard from him in weeks, and even then the calls were brief, garbled, raving pleas for money that ended when I put the phone down with a soft click, a humane death to his voice. It's like he's intuited how important this is for me, how potentially cleansing and healing, and he's made sure to inject his toxic presence. So much effort to find me, too. Vicki had mentioned where I was (why did I tell her? And she him?), and then he got online and scoured Levi's fansites and an aerial map for the compound's location. He was lost for a few hours on the twisty mountain roads but then found it—a miracle, he claims, another shimmering link on the chain of serendipity that includes the amazing story he's got to tell.

When I get back to the table, Dee is speaking in low, incantatory tones.

"The lights were flashing all around and I was so high that every one of them had tracers coming off it, as if I was walking under this glittery web. There was broken glass all around but I didn't notice it. This guy was laying there and people were screaming and running around and I guess—this is what people tell me later—that I walked up deadly calm and started performing CPR. We were so far out the cops were really slow getting there—this is Detroit, after all. I was giving compressions, like two hundred a minute, for ten minutes. This is almost humanly impossible. Some say it might be a world record. I didn't even realize what I was doing. I was so messed up I thought I was still in the club and this was some dance. I just kept going. It felt wonderful. I just remember seeing these lights going up and down and hearing this *click click* sound. That was the cartilage over the sternum, I'm told. The guy was certainly dead for most of that time. Then, right when help got there, he coughed, arched up under me, looked me in the eye. I just walked away and down the street . . . and all these people followed me, trying to thank me. They took me to the hospital with them and I slowly sobered up. The guy was alive. And here's the thing . . ."

Dee tries to catch my eye but I duck down and pet the dogs. "The thing is, when I felt that man—Miguel's—life return, something happened to me, too. I mean, I literally felt the force of my own life— before all the drugs and issues—leap back into me. I realized, then and there, that I would never use again. For real. And I haven't. Three weeks and going strong. It's like . . . not only did I restart Miguel's heart but my own."

Levi watches Dee with a twitching mouth that flicks into a small smile whenever Dee drives his story into a new absurdity. Of course they aren't absurdities to Levi. He's positively moved. When Dee falls silent, Levi springs forward, knocking down a salt shaker. "That is amazing, man. I have never heard anything more beautiful. You are so much like your Dad . . . you just have a way with words! God, Danny. I can't believe this kid!" He turns to me with his familiar look of awe (for what doesn't awe Levi?) and points from Dee to me and back. I shrug.

"He knows how to spin a tale," I say, echoing what the cops had said to me the first time I picked him up from an overnighter in jail.

After dinner, I head straight to my cabin, locking it in case Dee gets any ideas about dropping by for a little heart-to-heart. Then I call Natalie. She picks up right away, her voice sounding warm but a little edgy, as if whatever she's about to hear might require her to shift quickly into tough love. Natalie teaches in one of the worst schools in Detroit, where she is beloved and feared. There was a rumor going around that she reduced the superintendent to tears at a board meeting, then stopped anyone from offering him a Kleenex so he could experience the discomfort and filth his students did every day. This boldness is all the more disarming considering her face—pale, round, with an inexorable, stony quietude. Everything—from the way she kisses to the way she orders a bottle of wine—is done with a kind of resolute deliberateness, as if she'd considered the smoothest, truest way long before she had been called upon to act.

She listens for a few moments—but right when I'm getting to the nonsense about the CPR world record, she interrupts me.

"I don't think you should be putting this much energy toward him. Just don't engage. If you tell him to leave because he's on drugs, then he's got to stay to show you he's not. Attention will encourage him. Believe me, I know how this works. And it's not as if Dee has a long attention span anyway—remember what you told me about his landscaping business? He'll leave. Give it a few days."

She's probably right, but I don't like how she just rolls over the fact that I might be rattled at Dee's sudden appearance, especially when I'm just now feeling ready to song-write again. But Natalie's an emotional minimalist who doesn't need the gory details to read a situation correctly. And she's right about Dee—the landscaping idea, which occurred to him during a brief sober period, lasted less than twenty-four hours. He spent a solid twenty of those hours designing the tree logo that would go on his business cards—drawing and redrawing it in my living room, making it more and more fantastical and symbolic, using up every scrap of paper on a swirling design that incorporated the whole universe into a knothole in the tree's base. For years afterward I'd find them: a bird's nest scribbled on an old TV guide, a root system on a receipt, a bough creeping over the stamps in my passport.

The next morning, the first thing I hear upon waking is a high, squeaky warble and the sound of a lazily plucked guitar. I recognize that I'm-afraid-to-sing-for-real falsetto—Dee. And the guitar, Levi. The studio is next door to my cabin, and the unwelcome sounds come through the open window. I get up and see my computer is still open from last night, when I tried to verify Dee's story. Had he really set a world record for chest compression per minute and saved a man's life? But even if was true, did it matter? The ridiculous turns of his life seem like just more evidence of his addiction—it's like a stoner is writing his fate. I get out my notebook and try to remember some ideas I jotted down last night. After a while, Levi knocks on the door.

"Danny-boy, get up and jam with us! We're having a blast."

I step outside to talk to him.

"Look, Levi, I'm not going to jam with him. He's a junkie. I'm sorry he showed up here. You don't want to get invested in anything he does; he's not reliable. He needs to get back into rehab."

Levi looks me in the eye for a long moment. His gray hair stands up in a fuzzed swirl atop his head, like a novelty halo. He lifts his hand briefly and makes a loose cup around his ear, as if he misheard. Then he turns both hands up and speaks.

"Are you serious, Danny? Didn't you hear him last night? It sounds like he's over all that. Why not give him a chance?"

I can't blame Levi for being charmed—I've been there enough myself—but his words make me think he's unusually gullible. Dee's story was the kind of improbable drama that users cling to. Real recovery doesn't come from the flash-pop of some crazy encounter, and Levi should at least know that.

"Levi, I'm serious. You don't know him. He's just pretending. This is some ruse, some ploy to get into my good graces or get money or I don't even want to think about what he's trying to do. You don't know the history here—"

"Danny, let him stay here for now. Come on. We'll ask him to leave if something goes wrong, but otherwise? It might be fun! We've got plenty of room here. We need a young guy around to keep us two old goats fresh . . ."

Levi glances at the main house, where Lucinda, blue scarves streaming off her neck, bobs past the window like an exotic fish. "Dang it, Lucinda's waiting for me. Totally forgot! I'm supposed to take her to the garden this morning to harvest some stuff for tonight. Did you know we have a farm share down the road? It's a great place—the old guy named Gregors owns it. When he learned I was a rock star, he said that originally Woodstock was going to be on his property but the hippies got a bad vibe from his sheep, since they all were so well-behaved and lined up for their feed. They thought he was fascist and split . . ."

"Levi, I don't want to get into too much detail but Dee—"

"Hey, Danny, I've got to run. We'll talk later. Lucinda's giving me the eye. Women! You know what's scary? Watching her weed. Ever notice how aggressive women are about stuff like that? They can be all butterflies and rainbows but let them loose on dandelions and they become these focused little wildcats all claw, claw, claw . . ." He continues talking as he backs away, his step so light on the autumn leaves that he could be mistaken for a bounding squirrel.

It's not particularly to my son's credit that he's seduced Levi with his storytelling. Levi, for all his sophistication as a performer and musician, is a strangely guileless man, the kind of person whose brilliance, you might say, comes from that ability to be seduced, to emotionally connect with anyone and anything. No matter what he sings, he finds something beautiful and authentic within the words. I've always seen him as a kind of idiot savant, a brilliant, complex performer unburdened by actually being brilliant or complex.

Levi and I had a good string of hits from about 1973 to 1980. I'd even toured with him, generating new songs on the road. But by the eighties, our music had fallen out of favor, and we both used this as an opportunity to pursue other projects. Neither of us really recreated our early successes, but Levi did as well as an out-of-vogue folk rocker can reasonably expect, landing soundtrack work ("Cloud Tears" for that cartoon, "Davy Jones' Lockdown" for that ridiculous pirate/prison film). He elevated even that schlock to the point where I had tears in my eyes when I took my kids to see them and heard Levi singing over the credits. I did okay too, for a while, and landed on the adult contemporary chart with one forgettable tune. Then my career stalled out on one particular song I'd been hired to write for an up-and-coming neo-soul songstress. Her manager was looking for a simple Motown classic that would show off the girl's voice, but I became so taken with her tone and phrasing that I wanted to do something more ambitious, a little opus, a kind of Chapin's "Taxi" with a high-flying bridge. I wrote pages and pages, fifteen minutes worth of bittersweet sentiments (nothing the girl could have sung convincingly—she was just shy of twenty), wrote long past when the manager needed the lyrics, long past when the singer put out her first and last small-label album, long past when she gave up her music career and got into real estate (last I heard). I planned on finishing it for someone else—or for its own sake—but it never got done. The longer I worked the more tight and convoluted it became, and the simple thread of loss I hoped to convey became a hopeless tangle of abstraction and symbol that I tried to unweave for years before giving up.

Soon after that, Dee became a factor, and I just never got back to writing. I don't want that failed song to be the last work I do. I want to write like I used to—for a performer who really connects with my work, who can elevate and transform it. There's truly something magical in what Levi can do—when I hear my words in his voice, it's as if I can see a pathos in myself that I otherwise can't. It used to really help me.

Soon enough Dee himself stops by. I can tell it's him by the shave-and-a-haircut knock, a knock he never fails to use even when he's a total mess and hardly knows his own name. Strange what the mind holds onto when everything else is lost. When I open the door, he begins speaking in a fast blurt, as if he's memorized what he is going to say and needs to get it all out before he forgets.

"I know you don't believe me that I'm clean. I know you think I'm using even now, and I totally get that. I understand. But I am clean. I saved a guy's life. And he saved my life. I came here because I wanted you to know."

I let him in and sit down at my computer while he sits on the edge of the bed, rubbing his hands together and clearing his voice between sentences, waiting for me to say something.

"I truly believe some higher power put that man in front of me at the exact moment we both needed each other. I remember looking in his eyes and hearing the click when I did the compressions. His eyes were just dead. He was gone. I looked into those black holes and just coaxed the universe back. I brought myself back. It happened for a reason. Everything does. I believe me coming here and you being here and working with Levi—it's all part of a healing plan . . ."

Coaxed the universe back. I find myself typing the phrase without meaning to.

"Look, Dad, I'm sorry. For everything. But you have to believe what happened that night in Detroit was real—"

"From what I gathered, the 'uppers' you were on are what gave you the strength to do those chest compressions. Seems like a great argument for doing drugs, not for quitting. And I don't get, after all the shit you've done, why some freakout with a heart attack victim in the ghetto is what turned you around. What about all you did to me? How about the time you punched me and broke my glasses? Or when you cleared out my safe deposit box? None of that triggered an epiphany? And by the way, you still owe me that money . . ."

I keep going in this vein, though the whole while I'm picturing how I would have responded just a few years ago, and it is as if that self is next to me, getting up from the chair, embracing Dee, laughing and talking to him, reliving his heroism in Detroit, sharing funny stories about ditzy old Levi and speculating on Lucinda's relationship with him. I feel sorry for that ghost self—his fragile, temporary joys and more enduring disappointments—and relieved as hell that he's not me.

Dee cuts me off in a low cajoling voice, as if negotiating with an erratic mental patient. "Okay, okay, I understand you're still mad. I understand. But I'm going to show you. Believe it." He pats my shoulder as he leaves, and the gesture is infuriatingly paternal, as if I'm the troubled son.

Levi and I are outside the main house on the back porch, sipping wine at small café table. Lucinda has supplied a bowl of fruit, placing it down between us and then turning toward me as she left with what looked to me like a gently sardonic grin, the kind of playfully doubting look I've historically found sexy. She's probably overheard her share of absurd conversations out here—moldering rock stars measuring the weathers of their inner lives with Dopplers of crystals and cleansing diets and tomes written by this or that bestselling seer. Front men gone to seed who gossip with such desperation you'd think old grudges were the sole fuel of some inner sustaining furnace. There's no doubt a parade of eccentrics traipsing through here each summer, making music or art or pretending to.

The yard is scattered with bits of refuse used as both sculptures and as seating for friends of Levi who come here to work. A metal horse trough, flipped over and bleeding rust, sits next to an old tractor seat jammed into earth. A lizard made from bicycle chains rears up next to a kinetic sculpture of a large bird, its Plexiglas and pop-can-ring feathers vibrating lightly in the wind. I've been telling Levi all about Dee—the long history of drug abuse, the uncanny way he maintains his sobriety just long enough to earn your trust before he breaks it, etc., etc. Levi nods the whole time, his brow scrunched between his dusky blue eyes. Levi looks so sympathetic, so wise, that I almost expect a profound discourse on the breakdown of familial relationships vis-à-vis art, but then he scratches his brush of gray blond hair and pops a melon ball into his mouth.

"Well, Danny, all I can tell you is what I see. He seems like a great kid. We talked last night after you went to bed and he laid a lot of that heavy stuff out for me. Seems pretty self-knowing. We got to talking about the Zen concept of letting go . . . he's real bright, you know? He gives off a nice energy . . ."

The breeze moves Levi's hair away from his forehead, exposing his oddly dewy, luminous skin. His looks have always pulled from history—he can appear as rosy and sunstruck as a cherub in the clouds or as stiff and shadowed as a daguerreotype of a nineteenth-century colonel. His speaking voice—unguarded and rich, with the slightest vulnerable tremor on long vowels—makes whatever he says sound thoughtful. With Levi, I always find myself hearing him out, even though I'd cut someone else off with a scoff if I heard such palaver. He has a way of making reason itself seem cynical, something only the spiritually bankrupt need bother with.

I take a sip of wine. The dogs have been let out, and they walk out into the yard, stopping and posing among the yard art as if engaged in a challenging modern dance. Off in the distance I can see the light in Dee's cabin. Most likely he is packing up his things now, or walking in circles holding up his phone, trying to catch a signal from Detroit. Dee's inconsequential—coming to Chautauqua is about writing again, working with Levi to make something beautiful out of the pure belief of his voice.

"And that was a pretty amazing story about him saving that guy. You gotta believe his good karma is off the charts right about now."

I've spent the rest of the afternoon trying to write, without much luck. I asked Lucinda to bring dinner to me in my cabin, thinking it would be best to focus on my work rather than let Dee's dinner theater distract me. Who knows what the next installment will be? Maybe he rescued a baby at the bottom of a lake, buoyed by a few hits of nitrous oxide. But the less I engage the better, and now the thought of returning my plates to Lucinda as the evening winds down gives me something to work toward. When she dropped off my food, she tapped my forearm with her small silver-ringed hand and told me not to work too hard. That was nice.

Nothing's come so far; the page in front of me is still empty. I think about calling Natalie, but her hyperpracticality wouldn't be useful now. She wouldn't understand what was going on here anyway— the skillful way I'm juggling Levi's sensibilities with Dee's presence wouldn't register with her. Subtleties don't interest her—the broad strokes do—will this student pass, is this student off drugs, how can I keep this one from getting pregnant. Good for her line of work, but not for art.

I write out a phrase—*the stars are a scrolling readout*—and I start to relax. It's a good line, good enough to perhaps build something from it. Then it hits me. This is a Dee phrase. He called a few months ago and started talking about how the stars seemed like some kind of electric readout, describing his state of mind as he wandered down the beach. I immediately scratch it out, bearing down on the paper so even the contours of the words can't be seen. I'm breathing hard and I put my hand on my heart and feel it flutter. I take a drink from the chilled white wine Lucinda so thoughtfully left, then I try again.

I watched her aurora eyes . . . Not so good, but okay, a start. I put my pen to my lips and concentrate on the line, thinking of where to take it next. Then I remember. Dee said this one when he called to describe his breakup with his waifish girlfriend, the one with the shoots-n-ladders tattoo that covered her whole left leg, winding from her ankle all the way up to the exposed white pockets of her cut-off shorts, and I presume, beyond. She was blinking out after a binge of some sort, and Dee had stayed up watching her, willing her mind to change about their future. This time I scribble the words out so roughly that the paper tears. I rip the whole sheet off and start with a fresh one.

By the flipped silhouette, I regained a planet in you, the shimmer of relief . . . It keeps happening. Everything reveals itself as Dee's. It's as if his lovely phrases have colonized my mind and pushed everything out. I don't want to use these words. I don't want any part of Dee in this work. The whole point is to move fully past all that. Back to the time before the kid was even born. But it's as if, through some sinister telepathy, Dee keeps interrupting. I try writing terrible phrases, stupid things, or just gibberish. No dice. Everything seems to pull from something Dee once slurred, mumbled, or shouted. There's not an unsullied thought in my head.

I haven't touched my food—some kind of thick pasta with flecks of fish grows cold next to me. I take another drink. Dinner is probably over by now. I could return my plates, talk with Lucinda and commiserate about the crazy talk she is forced to bear witness to around here. That look of hers—quiet, ironic, and warm—makes it clear that she has a high sense of the absurd, no doubt honed by watching Levi and the excesses that unfold around him. We could have a glass of wine and laugh at the strangeness of our companions. That will be as good for her, I'm sure, as it will be for me.

I leave the cabin and see that the studio light is on, as if Levi and Dee might be getting together for a postdinner session. Fine, fair enough. I fling the dinner off my plate into the woods. Wouldn't want to offend Lucinda with an unfinished dinner. It's dark and somewhat chilly. The crisp margins of the half-moon above look like a surgical excision in the night, a bright wedge of proud flesh. It's incredibly quiet, except for the dampened bustle of nocturnal animals waking and beginning their rounds. And a long squeak, a curse and a laugh—something being moved in the studio, someone stubbing a toe.

Lucinda joins me for a drink in the dining room. The lights are all dimmed, and a candle, still burning from dinnertime, weeps wax between us. She's lovely in this light. Her face is wide at the top, with large, heavily lidded eyes, while her mouth is small and overstuffed with a jumble of teeth, the sliver of an overbite showing even when she shuts her lips. A messy dark braid falls over her shoulder. She's the type of woman who seems ageless—there's no trace of youthful plumpness in the flat planes her face, nor is there a wrinkle. She tells me about her life in a small village in Portugal, her culinary schooling in the States, and a story about smuggling saffron in the lining of her bra on a flight after a visit home. When she laughs her rumbly low laugh, she shakes her head and winces, as if being amused is a little painful, something to shake off.

"Listen," I finally say, when we've both relaxed sufficiently. "What do you think of these two jokers? I mean, I love Levi, don't get me wrong, but we both know he's kind of a flake. And my son Dee—sorry he's here by the way—I did *not* invite him—I give you credit for not laughing and spitting up your wine when he was going on about restarting that bum's heart and his 'own heart as well ...'"

I start to laugh myself now, wild peals. My eyes are filling with tears and a little bubble of hysteria, pleasurable and frightening, rises in my chest. I touch Lucinda's wrist to ground myself, to keep myself in the room and of this world. The warmth of her skin sobers me up, and I look at her, giving her a chance to let loose her own commentary and pained chuckle.

"I'm not sure I know what you mean. Levi is a bright man. And your son . . . his story was amazing. I don't know why a person would laugh at that."

Is she putting me on? Or simply making me disassemble the whole myth that Dee built around his addiction as a kind of flirtation? I laugh, to show Lucinda I'm onto her, and then comply. I tell her his story is unbelievable, full of logical holes and crazy claims, and even if it was true, Dee's supposed epiphany and conversation struck me as cheap, sudden, and deluded. All that talk of destiny—destiny is just narcissism, a sad wish that the events of the world all ordered themselves around you. As I'm sure Lucinda knows.

"I'm not sure about all that. Some strange things are true. When I was a young girl in Barroselas, we had a saying, 'The water flows without cease.' It means your life is traveling somewhere, somewhere beyond your control. On birthdays we'd make a chain of flowers, drop it in the river, then spend the whole day following where it floated. If the chain got snagged, we would have a picnic on the bank and wait for it to either break apart or get free. It was said that the snag meant your year would be difficult and it was always right. I got the snag the year my fiancé found his Spanish girlfriend. I was so angry I cooked up everything we had in the pantry and left seven full meals on the porch. But you, maybe you don't think this way. You seem to be more of a business type person? A person who follows only facts and maybe money. That's how you talk."

So there will be no meeting of the minds. I put my head down on the table for a moment, and let the room swim. Lucinda pats my head and walks out, the dogs heaving up with a joint sigh and following her out. The sink runs and pans clang and then the kitchen light goes out. Eventually, I get up. I have the space to myself. I walk around, a little drunk, peering at all Levi's souvenirs and tchotchkes. With all the traveling he's done, you'd think he'd develop some street smarts, some healthy self-protection.

I think of what Dee would do alone in a big, opulent space like this. *Steal.* He would steal to feed his habit, steal out of some misguided attempt to balance out the scales of life. "You're rich," he had once said to me, after pawning off James Taylor's signed set list for something he instantly shot or inhaled into his body. "You didn't need it. It was just a fucking museum piece, morgue décor." He's stolen thousands of dollars' worth of things from me over the years, stole so much that I changed my locks every few months as a matter of course. When he'd visit I'd follow him to the bathroom. I'd make sure he was wearing short sleeves, and I'd even ask him to empty his pockets in front of me when he left, which he'd do with a baneful expression, like some pauper cartoon character.

Dee would steal. He probably already has. Levi is so innocent, so easily duped . . . There's something both inspirational and unseemly in Levi's openness, his willingness to trust all things. In a young man, it seems right and normal, but in Levi that innocence—suspended perfectly intact like some primordial bug in amber—feels spooky, unreal. How is it that he hasn't changed at all? The bubble of fame can't account for it. He was swindled out of money, swindled out of the rights to some of the best songs in his catalogue by Larry Devins, his manager in the eighties. He's been through at least two divorces, as far as I know. His father was a harsh military man who thought his son's dreams of a life in music were corrupt and delusional, and the man died right before we left on our first tour, before Levi could say "I told you so." Dee would take him for everything he had.

My eyes fall on a small jade elephant, a trinket from Levi's trip to India when he was in his full Buddhist phase. As I think of Dee and

Levi—both so deluded in their own way, both so unreasonable—I pick up the figurine and switch it from hand to hand. The cool stone feels pleasant, bracing, as if it were a physical representation of the clarity that everyone in Chautauqua seems to lack. Idly, I move through the house with it, looking at old pictures of Levi and old pictures of me. Then I pocket it.

The next morning Dee and Levi are at the table, talking about something they keep referring to as "the secret weapon." I eat my oatmeal and watch the empty spot where the jade elephant had been. No one seems to notice.

"I can't wait to try out the secret weapon, man. I think you are totally right on that it'll make that track." Levi is saying to Dee.

Then he turns to me. "Danny, you've got to come to the studio. You gotta hear what Dee and I came up with. We've got an incredible track, ninety percent done, we just need lyrics. Would you give a listen? I know you've been working on the lyrics . . . maybe you can match them up with what we got so far."

I follow them into the studio, the place I've been avoiding since I arrived. Levi's walk is unchanged—eager and upright, he seems to rise up on tiptoe, as if trying to take a peek at something each stride. Dee walks with a measured, quiet step, like a contemplative monk walking the grounds, his hands clasped behind his back. Far different from the darting, manic boy who was constantly jiggling a leg or running his hands through his hair.

Levi hands me the headphones and for a moment I hear nothing. Then the music comes in. Something like a muted toy xylophone reverbing. Then, Levi's voice, strangely lilting, then falling into spoken word. Improvised placeholder lyrics and a vaguely Spanish guitar hook, and then some kind of clicking dirtied up the track. The tick becomes louder but remains muffled, like sticks snapping under a coat of leaves. Then, the guitar, this time more muscular, rising up and thinning out to a clear high sound that I feel in my teeth, like a tuning fork. And the tick, quieting. I pull the headphones off.

"What do you think?" Levi leans forward and looks me in the eye. Dee stands over his shoulder and seems to be meditating, humming to himself with his eyes closed.

"Interesting. A real departure. What's that ticking sound that starts midway? It was distracting."

Levi smiles and looks back over his shoulder at Dee, who breaks into a wide grin. Then Levi laughs and slaps my knee.

"That's the secret weapon. That sound . . . it's the click of a compressed sternum during CPR. Dee found the sample from some emergency training web video. Isn't it amazing? That sound is just so . . . I don't know . . . guttural or something. Fleshy. Bony. I love it. It's full of life, huh?"

I have quite a bounty in my pocket. The jade elephant from earlier, the sea horse ring, a brass swan incense holder, my own watch, and the ultimate prize—one of Levi's and my gold records, slipped into the lining of my coat. It all clinks and chimes in my coat like frolicsome imps playing atonal music. I'm wandering all around Chautauqua, halfway looking for Lucinda and halfway plotting how to deal with Dee. And halfway—if I can have another halfway here—just enjoying the act of roaming around with all these thoughts and desires in my head, things no one knows about. Levi thinks I'm a blocked writer at odds with my perfectly nice son. Dee thinks I'm just stewing in my cabin, on the cusp of breaking down and believing him once more, opening my heart and wallet as butterflies of acceptance and love flutter about both our faces. And Lucinda thinks I'm a cynic, a killer of mysteries, and probably a dull guy besides, compared to sweet celestial

Levi. But I'm not those things. If Lucinda saw me now, she'd see that I was electric with possibility. The taken objects—and the soft clamor of their physical presence—makes me feel a sudden confidence, a confidence that can come only when you hold something back from the world. Dee used to talk about the pleasures of a secret high when he was younger, that wonderful feeling of being stoned while no one knows or can tell. Extra points if you're doing something exceptionally wholesome like cooking Christmas cookies with grandma. The swirls and shifts of the room—the wild non sequitur thoughts—these are all your own to savor and conceal.

I turn off into the woods. Bars of light bend over the high branches and thin as they focus in on the forest floor. This is wild country—there are no trails, and *Rosa multiflora* keeps snagging me, like a clutch of fans desperate for whatever piece of me they can get. The hillside seems repetitive and smudged; nature seems to me a dull pattern, a decorative border. It's steep, and I slide on my heels a few times. An enormous rotted log, mossy and covered with the sinewy trails of some boring insect, lies across the way. It's split in the middle, right down to the ground. I pull the record out of my coat lining and take a look at it. It's the gold record for "Many a Moon." The frame includes the silver-painted record, the little certifying plaque from the RIAA and a photograph of Levi and me, riding double on a statue Civil War horse on tour long ago. I sat in front of the general, and he sat behind, hugging the stone figure with what appeared to be a rush of affection.

It was an unexpected hit for us. The song used lunar imagery to describe the way a man and a women drift apart and back together. *She kept me waiting on her half-lit eyes . . .* As I wrote the thing I imagined Levi and me laughing over it over a joint, wadding it up and tossing it in the busted base drum we used as a trash can. Levi had no high sense of irony, I knew, but even he would find this an occasion to roll his eyes and drop, for a moment at least, his blinding sincerity. I kept writing, pushing the lyrics into schmaltz and sugar, to baroque despair, and then, finally, an unearned and soaring end. I felt strange and elated when I handed Levi my work. He laughed just a little, said "crazy, Danny," then began to play and sing. He mugged and oversang for a few bars then let the thing fall into a kind of weird hiccupping tone, something between crying and laughing, a lovely kind of thing that kept the eye-rolling in it as well as that overarching sense that it mattered.

I pop the record out of the frame. The photo of Levi and me flutters off. I push the record into the groove in the wood. The last quarter inch or so protrudes and catches the light. I put my hands in the dirt, pull up some moss and leaves, and spread it over the edge of the record. Done and done. I break down the frame, throw the glass at a tree, kick earth on the shards.

Levi will surely notice it is gone and I already have my reaction planned. I will simply turn to Dee with a sad look, a look of deep disappointment, a look of fragile trust broken. I'll hold up my wrist and show that my watch, too, is gone. Dee will start rolling out his denials, and Levi, watching the tableaux, will see what Dee truly is—a charmer, a fraud, a spinner of tales. I want to hear his sputtering denial, see the confusion break over his face. Of course it's true that he didn't actually steal the thing, but small matter. It will give him a little taste of what it feels like to talk to him during one of his binges. The way a word in the conversation would suddenly slide off the rational, and you'd know. Every time he called and at least started the conversation with "Hello," I used to be filled with hope, since so many of his calls began midstream in what best resembled the jump cuts and shorthand of an inner monologue, as if you were simply a microphone he switched on in his brain.

I turn and run up the hill, tromping over brambles, letting others snag me and spin me around for a moment. I leap over a log into a tangle of vines and fall onto my back. The wind is knocked out of me, and I look up at the little lacework of sky through the trees, waiting on my breath. Actually, it feels like I'm waiting to breathe out, not in.

It's fine I can't write anymore, I think, enjoying the breathless silence of my own body. What's the big obsession with letting things out into the world? Songs, ideas, stories . . . the real pleasure is keeping it all in. That's where the power is.

When I get up, gasping, I continue racing up the hill where Lucinda, as if fated, stands watching the dogs sniff and poop amongst the trash sculptures. Her back, draped in a golden camel cape, seems to nod and beckon as she pets one of the strange, stilted dogs. I swoop behind her and do the least expected thing: lift her up and spin her, watching her face go ashen and then, with enough revolutions, a shocking red.

"And how is the writing going? And what's happened with Dee?" Natalie asks. She sounds so aggressively no-nonsense that I half expect all of Chautauqua to crumble into the void as she talks, the house lights to flick back on, and real life to resume. Her voice in this atmosphere is completely out of place; there's nothing I could say that would make sense to her now, and nothing she could say that would be relevant here. You always get into these moments with lovers, though, and you learn to cloak experience with bland chatter rather than try to convey the impossible.

"The writing's tough. I've taken a lot of time off, as you know, but I'm slowly warming up again. Dee's still here but laying low. It's fine. I'm not letting him get to me."

I walk around the cabin as I talk and peer in the closet. A hefty pile of objects now, from both the main house and the studio. I smile when I see the bejeweled dog collar at the top of the pile. I slipped it off as one of beasts trotted by, so smoothly that it didn't even break stride.

"And you?" I ask, as I sit down at my desk. I flip my notebook open, where I've now written every interesting phrase Dee has ever said during a binge. Dozens have come to me in the last hours. I figure if I write them all down, then cross them all out, I might purge my brain of them, too. It feels good to scratch over them. As good as any writing session.

Natalie tells me all about a student of hers—a brilliant girl, gifted in math, whose boyfriend is a notorious neighborhood thug. This girl, Olivia, keeps playing hooky. The mother's doing nothing. Natalie drives into the girl's block and confronts the girl's mother in the street. Words are exchanged. It's unprofessional viewed one way, viewed another it is absolutely necessary . . . My mind drifts as she talks—*words are exchanged*—the cliché seems weirdly apropos, as it describes what's happened with Dee's old phrases. He's given me his words and taken all of mine.

I let Natalie talk, let her feel as if we're sharing something. Then I tell her I love her and goodbye.

When Levi, Lucinda, and Dee all appear at my cabin door, I assume they're inviting me to dinner—insisting that I come out, take a break from all the work. The second possibility is that they've confronted Dee about his stealing and are dragging him to me, like wardens, so I can pass the final judgment on him. I keep my face neutral so I can be ready for either possibility. Levi asks if they can come in, and I step aside. They all file in—Dee and Lucinda sit on the bed, Levi in the corner rocking chair and I sit at my desk.

Levi clears his throat and rearranges himself in the chair several times. Lucinda keeps her profile to me, her eyes on Levi. She's wearing what looks like one long rose-colored scarf, wrapped multiple times around her body to make a dress. I get the feeling if I grabbed one end and pulled, her whole person would unravel and I'd be standing there, holding nothing but a bolt of limp fabric. Dee's skin is sheened with sweat, and a few strands of his hair cling to his hairline in even swoops, like crown molding. He seems to be sitting in a position to best show off his "ink." His wrists are turned up so the trust tattoo shows. His right leg is crossed over his left, and his jeans ride up so the roots of the tree on his calf can be seen, reaching down into his sockless tennis shoes. The small picket fence on his collarbone pokes through a gap in his collar. A strange tattoo—is it a commentary on the emptiness of suburban striving? Does it indicate that he's within the fence—trapped—or that we, the onlookers, are the ones trapped, and *he's* actually on the outside, in some more authentic bohemian beyond? He swallows hard and the pickets rise up for a moment.

"Danny, we're here because . . ." Levi coughs and scratches his neck. He takes a few breaths. The yellow wood of the cabin reflects a gold light on his colorless hair; he looks like a beatific stained-glass saint, complete with the weepy eyes. He jumps up from his chair and gestures with both hands.

"I just want to say, right off, that this isn't about *the stuff*, you know? Material things—they've never meant shit to me, you know that, right Danny? That's not what this is about. It's about you know, just why? What's going on with you? If you want something, just ask. You're my friend. I want to give you things. You've gotta know that. So why the secretive stuff?"

I look at Dee, who is rubbing his wrists together and looking at the ceiling.

"What secretive stuff?"

"Well, gee Danny. The taking things. You've been taking things. Lucinda says you've been walking around the house late at night, just grabbing stuff, I guess . . ."

"Wait." I get up and step towards Dee, standing over him. "You're calling me a thief? When this guy's skulking around the property? Here's your problem. This kid. He's causing trouble. Stealing and pinning it on his dad. It's not the first time he's pulled this kind of shit. This is what he does."

"Goddamnit, Dad," and now Dee is up, right in my face. Lucinda is up too, her hand on him, and I can hear her begging him to be calm, murmuring some mantra about quiet waters. "I haven't done anything, Dad, and you know it. You've got the problem, you—"

And then Levi rushes over to break us apart. He's moving fast, and then he's down at our feet. We all crouch down. All six hands are on him, trying to flip him over but pulling him opposite directions. Then he's over, face up. His eyes are filmed over and his face, without the girding of his permanent smile, flattens and pools.

I used to think of emergencies as these character-galvanizing events, these moments when life does a casting call and shows a person for who they truly are. The timid and mousy become commanding heroes, barking instructions, and the brash in everyday life shrink into impotence and hysteria. So once the situation becomes plain—that Levi is in very bad shape, and that an ambulance will have a hell of time getting out here in time, meaning we have to drive—I watch as I'm moved, as if by the impatient hands of a director, into the role of the stunned, incoherent bystander, whose every move is an impediment and liability. I can't take my eyes off of Levi, who is in and out of consciousness on the floor. I feel like the whole problem is my perception, and if I could just bring Levi into better focus—make some sense of his moaning, reassemble his sliding features back into their familiar formation of gentle, pleased bemusement, all would be solved.

Lucinda and Dee are speaking in short, efficient barks to one another. Dee grabs my shoulder and pushes me back.

"Dad, Dad! Does your car have gas?"

I tell him yes, and I can hear, in my voice, a scary sluggishness as I'm now on Levi time, the slow-down of catastrophe. Dee shakes me, pulls me up, and the two of us lift and halfway drag Levi to the car. The sun is Indian-summer bright, and the slight heat brings out flavors in the woods—musky animal hair, the yeast of last year's thickening leaves, the ferment of overripe berries. The incongruent outdoors makes our carrying of Levi seem celebratory, a triumphant king paraded around by his footmen. We get to the car, and Dee morphs into an engineer, an expert in all the ways an inert body can be arranged into the tight space of a midsize sedan's back seat. He delivers rapid fire orders, tells me where to grab Levi, the pounds of pressure I should apply to each pull.

"Sit with Levi. Keep his head up so he doesn't choke. If he stops breathing, yell out. Got it?"

I climb in and prop myself against Levi's listing body. He turns his head and flutters his hands toward me. The car screeches away from Chautauqua, down the steep dirt road with all the switchbacks. Lucinda sedately narrates the route while Dee pilots the car, his eyes fixed and flat in the rear view mirror.

Levi falls onto me. Each of his breaths barely strings to the next. His head is on my lap, his eyes flutter back and forward. Expressions appear—slight smiles, squints, a pop of surprise widening his eyes and mouth—then depart, erasing more of his face as they go, like a wiping hand. I put my hands on either side of him, trying to keep him still, but his head feels like it's losing mass, emptying with each of his rough breaths, as if breathing were draining his substance rather than sustaining it. My own breath shortens and I feel the clutch of panic around my heart, something I last felt running around the city looking for Dee, sure that a pile of rags and fast food bags was his dead body. Even when it wasn't, I slid to the ground, cutting my palms on glass and junk all around me, huffing in short shallow breaths like some dog, frantically sniffing the life out of some primo scent. I focused on the creased and warped image of a cartoon dolphin on a McDonald's bag, the kind of bland commercial image that doesn't admit of life or death or anything, until I was finally able to get up.

Dee hears my breathing, and so does Lucinda. Dee catches my eyes in the mirror.

"It's okay, Dad. He'll be fine. People can look really bad and be okay. Just stay calm. That's your only job right now."

The car bounces and rolls. I put my arm over Levi and hold him. Dee turns on the radio. It's one of our songs—Levi's and mine—that I'd been listening to on the way to Chautauqua. Levi's voice fills the car. He sounds both melancholy and luxurious, like someone blinking tears back and smiling into a warm sun. The song is "When We Turn Away," a lament I wrote after my breakup with Joyce.

> And when we turn away
> I see all the city lights
> the beach we never made it to
> the flowered dress I thought of buying you . . .

Dee begins singing, in a buttery tenor, a voice I've never heard before, a voice perhaps reserved for those moments when no one is listening closely. Lucinda joins in with a bright soprano with a shrill edge, a dangerous voice that soars and shears. And then I'm singing, very quietly, in a little flat drone. I'm a bad singer with terrible pitch—that's why I'm the lyricist—and I can't recall the last time I sang, even to myself. I don't ever sing my own words. But it helps me breathe. Each note is making me exhale a little longer, each pause cues me to breathe in.

The road gets rougher, and we're pitched into a series of blind turns. Dee stops singing. His forearms are so tense on the wheel that they shiver. I'm in no shape or position to offer comfort, but I want to say something.

"This is the worst part. Just this part of not knowing what's going to happen. I think hell is waiting to know if you're going to hell or not. The waiting's the hell."

"Dad, that's about the least comforting thing you could say." He catches my face in the mirror and shakes his head. Lucinda chuckles as if she's just smashed her finger.

Levi blinks up at me, recognition lapping over his face and receding. His voice, even in this ragged whisper, sounds sure.

"It's still a good line."

THE FLANNERY O'CONNOR AWARD FOR SHORT FICTION